"What do you want, Mace?" Rhett's question was soft, guarded.

She skewed her lips to the side as if trying to find the right words. "I'm just wondering where the boy I knew went."

Rhett crossed his arms. "He grew up."

"That's a pity," Macy said. "He had this amazing ability to dream big, but plan well—something this place really needs. That boy could have shaped the ranch into something beyond what his father possibly ever could have."

He clenched his teeth and reminded himself that Macy was just being Macy. She'd been known to kick a hornets' nest before—literally.

He pressed his palms against the armrests. "You finished?"

"For now, sure. Forever?" she asked. "Not a chance."

Rhett couldn't hold in a chuckle. "I don't doubt it one bit."

This was the Macy he remembered, *his* Macy— someone who would stand against the wind and glare at a coming storm. Someone who didn't flinch.

Well, not his Macy. He wasn't quite sure where that thought had come from…

Avid reader, coffee drinker and chocolate aficionado **Jessica Keller** has degrees in communications and biblical studies and spends too much time on Instagram and Pinterest. Jessica calls the Midwest home. She lives for fall, farmers' markets and driving with the windows down. To learn more, visit Jessica at www.jessicakellerbooks.com.

Visit the Author Profile page at Harlequin.com for more titles.

The Rancher's Legacy

Jessica Keller

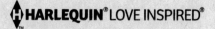

Recycling programs
for this product may
not exist in your area.

 LOVE INSPIRED BOOKS

ISBN-13: 978-1-335-53911-3

The Rancher's Legacy

Copyright © 2019 by Jessica Koschnitzky

www.Harlequin.com

Printed in U.S.A.

For the ladies in my *Psalms* 23 study.
Thanks for being my sisters.
Thanks for yanking me back on the path.
Thank you for being there. Always.

He restoreth my soul: he leadeth me in the paths of righteousness for his name's sake. Yea, though I walk through the valley of the shadow of death, I will fear no evil: for thou art with me; thy rod and thy staff they comfort me.

—*Psalms* 23:3–4

Chapter One

"I don't know why you're here." Rhett Jarrett rested his elbows on the large desk. It was too large—too grand—and he'd never look right behind it. Never be able to fill the spot his dad had. "I mean, other than it's always nice to see you. But you know where I stand on this."

Uncle Travis pushed more papers across the desktop. "With time, maybe you'll see his reasoning."

Rhett opened a drawer and slid the papers unceremoniously inside. Rereading the will wouldn't suddenly make him appreciate the choices his father had made. All it would serve to do was remind Rhett his dad had found a way to control him after the grave.

Late afternoon sunshine poured through the wide windows filling the west-facing wall of the office. March had begun unseasonably warm, even by Texas standards.

Upon entering the office a few minutes ago, Rhett had immediately cracked a few of the windows in an attempt to banish the musty odor of too many papers and books collecting dust in one cramped place. No doubt the wood paneling lining the lower half of the walls hadn't helped his mood either. It only seemed to add to the dark heaviness that had settled on Rhett's life since his dad's sudden passing. Unsaid words, missed opportunities and apologies that would never happen weighed him down.

No amount of fresh air would clear his chest of those things.

Air gusted in, carrying with it the smells of the horses in the nearest enclosure and the cattle in the pastures beyond. They mingled with the scents of Texas Indian paintbrush, bluebonnets and red poppies. Wildflowers quilted the fields on either side of the long driveway leading to his family's property. Spring at the ranch had always been his favorite time of year. He liked the physical parts of the ranch—the animals, the fields, the work.

Just not all the *other* aspects of Red Dog Ranch.

Not the parts his dad had cared about.

"Uncle Travis, listen. I—" Rhett started.

The door to the office clicked open and Macy Howell appeared in the doorway. With her hand resting on the knob, she hesitated for a few seconds. Her long, black hair swayed from her abrupt stop.

Rhett had known he would see his dad's office assistant sooner or later, but after the last few years of carefully visiting Red Dog Ranch only when he had been assured she was busy or away from the property…it was startling to see her so soon his first day in the office.

Macy adjusted the armful of files she clutched. Her gaze hit the floor like a dropped quarter. "I didn't realize you were busy. Should I come back later?"

But Macy casting down her eyes didn't compute for Rhett. Growing up, she'd been the girl who would spit at a wildfire and dare it to come closer. She'd hauled hay bales in the field at the same pace as Rhett and his brothers had.

When Rhett had scooped Macy into his arms after she'd been bitten by a copperhead, she had told him not to worry because the pit viper had barely kissed her. Even in that sort of pain, she'd been focused on being tough and making others feel better.

The Macy Howell he knew didn't hesitate, didn't look away.

She especially didn't look *down*.

The back of Rhett's neck prickled in a way that made him want to scrub at it. He fought the urge to ask her what was wrong. But they'd stopped asking each other prying questions three years ago. One kiss had changed everything.

Ruined everything.

And he shouldn't care.

Didn't care.

He dug his fingers into his knees.

Kodiak, Rhett's seventy-pound Chesapeake Bay retriever, lifted her giant head and sniffed in Macy's direction. The dog lazily looked back at Rhett as if to ask if this person was a threat.

Oh, she was.

With a gaze that could melt his resolve and her bright smile, Macy definitely was.

Satisfied that Rhett hadn't given a command, Kodiak let out a loud harrumph and laid her head back down. Her front paws stretched so the tips dipped into a spear of sunlight.

Despite Macy seeming to act out of character, the sight of her standing there in jeans and a flannel over a blue T-shirt still hit Rhett with the force of a double-strength energy drink spiked with strong coffee. She had a pencil tucked behind her ear. She looked like…like the best friend she'd once been. Like the person he used to be able to count on.

Like someone who hadn't rejected him.

Looks could be deceiving.

Uncle Travis's bushy gray eyebrows rose as if to ask, "Are you going to answer her, or what?"

Rhett cleared his throat, but it felt as if he'd swallowed a mouthful of summer soil that had baked in the Texas sun for weeks on end. Gritty and dry. "What do you need?"

"These are the files for the teens with internships starting this weekend. You should probably look them over. Know something about each one before you have to train them." She stepped into the room holding the pile of file jackets like a peace offering. "Brock always did."

Brock Jarrett, also known as his father.

Rhett's shoulders stiffened. "There's no one else set up to train them? Dad did it all?"

"I don't think Brock had made plans in case…" Uncle Travis's voice drifted away.

In case he died suddenly.

In case a trip to the library became his last trip.

In case one uninsured teenager sending a text while driving changed thc Jarrett family forever.

Macy took another step into the room. "He usually spent the first few days with them, yes. They each get assigned to a staff member, but Brock did the bulk of the mentoring."

Rhett shook his head. "Someone else can do it."

Kodiak groaned and lifted her head, alerted to trouble by his change in tone.

Macy's wide brown eyes searched his. "Rhett." She whispered his name and, for a reason he didn't want to explore, it made his gut hurt. "Please."

Rhett let his gaze land on the painting of longhorns instead of Macy. Meeting her pleading eyes made his resolve shaky and that was the last thing he wanted. His mom had painted the picture years ago, before her mind had begun to fail her. She'd proudly given it to Brock as a Valentine's day gift.

Thinking of his mom made Rhett sit a little

straighter. Her well-being depended on how he ran this ranch now. The will clearly stated Rhett was to take care of her and provide stable jobs for his sister, Shannon; Cassidy, the girl-friend of his deceased brother, Wade; Wade's daughter, Piper; and his brother, Boone, and his family. With Boone off at seminary with his wife and daughter, at least that responsibility was off Rhett's list. But the others stood.

However, so did the will's ironclad wording about the ranch continuing to serve foster kids. If Rhett put a stop to the foster programs at Red Dog Ranch, the will stated he would have to forfeit his inheritance. It was continue his dad's work or get none of it.

"Leave them on the table." Rhett jerked his chin toward a small side table near the office door.

Macy did, but she stayed in the doorway. "We need to talk about the spring kickoff event and the Easter egg hunt."

"Put those thoughts on hold. I'm looking into cancelling programs," Rhett said as he turned back to his uncle. "Which means you and I need to keep talking."

Macy's eyes narrowed for a second. She was biting her tongue. Years of knowing her made that clear, but she backed out of the room and closed the door.

As Rhett waited for his uncle to say something, he rubbed his thumb back and forth over an etching near the bottom right edge of the desktop. His dad had made him muck stalls alone for two weeks straight after Rhett had carved the indentation. At all of seven or eight years old, it had been quite a chore.

Uncle Travis offered a tight smile. "She's the perfect one to work with to help you meet the terms of the will. You see that, don't you?"

Rhett pinched the bridge of his nose.

Of course he saw that.

It was half the problem.

Macy had always put the foster programs before everything else, just like Brock had. Before the moneymaking aspects of the ranch, before family, before friendships. She had a passion and knowledge Rhett lacked, but working alongside her would be difficult; between losing his dad, dealing with family drama and being forced to put his business on hold to deal with Red Dog Ranch, Rhett was already past his ears in difficult. He needed to start making hard decisions and taking action to mitigate losses and stress.

Keeping a wide berth from Macy was one significant way to limit stress.

"As executor, don't you have the power to change the stipulations?"

His uncle's shoulders drooped with a sigh. "We've been over this."

And they had.

Many times.

As executor, Travis's job was to make certain all of Brock Jarrett's wishes were carried out to the letter. And Rhett's father had left many...letters. Red Dog Ranch had been willed to Rhett in full—the land and his father's vast accounts. But there were conditions.

If Rhett rejected the position of director, then they were supposed to sell the land and donate the money from the sale to a charity Brock had stipulated. Even in death his dad had placed continuation of the programs offered at the ranch before his family's long-term well-being. The only other option allowed in the will was for the property to pass to Boone, but Boone had been emphatic about refusing the inheritance. He wanted to finish seminary. He had a plan that didn't involve the ranch and no one could fault Boone for putting God first.

Well, Rhett refused to remove his mom from her home, from the land she loved. Even at the expense of his own happiness. His father had effectively tied his hands, making him the bad guy if he backed out.

Rhett lifted his chin. He wasn't backing out. He would take care of his family's future, would succeed in a way his father never had.

Kodiak made a small sound in her sleep, drawing Rhett's attention for a heartbeat.

He had placed his business, Straight Arrow Retrievers, on hold after getting the call that his father had passed away. But "on hold" might quickly become "closed forever." A burning sensation settled in Rhett's chest.

It was too much to manage. Too much to juggle. There was no way he could keep his business, the ranch and the foster programs all running successfully. One of them had to go.

His jaw hardened. "I'm going to find a loop-hole out of the foster programs at the ranch."

Uncle Travis frowned. "Even if you could—and I'm fairly certain you can't—talk like that would have broken your dad's heart."

"He knew how I felt about everything when he chose this for me," Rhett said.

While Red Dog Ranch had always func-tioned as a working cattle ranch, it also existed as a place that served children in the foster sys-tem. When Rhett was young, they had started hosting large parties for foster kids throughout Texas Hill Country for every major holiday. That had morphed into weekend programs that taught horseback riding and other life skills. The final addition had been building a summer camp on the property that was free for foster children to attend.

The summer camp had been Brock's pride and joy. It had seemed as if he lived all year for the weeks the ranch swelled with hundreds of kids. His father had poured his time and energy into every single one of the kids. Often as kids aged out of the foster care system, Brock had offered them positions on his property.

Rhett cared about kids who didn't have a home.

He did.

But it would be almost impossible to carry on his dad's mission with the same passion. He scrubbed his hand over his jaw and blew out a long breath. As horrible as it sounded, he resented Red Dog Ranch and all that it stood for. His father had cared more about it and the foster children than anything else.

Especially more than he'd cared about Rhett.

Uncle Travis clicked his briefcase closed and stood up. He hovered near the desk, though. "A gift is only as good as what you do with it."

Rhett stood. Crossed his arms over his chest. "A gift and a burden are two very different things."

But Uncle Travis pressed on. "Your aunt Pearl, bless her, she never knew what to do when someone gave her something really nice." He laid his free hand over his heart. "When I lost her and got around to cleaning out her stuff, you know what I found?"

Rhett pressed his fingertips into the solid desktop and shook his head. Once Uncle Travis got started down a rabbit trail, there was no point stopping him.

"Boxes of expensive lotions and perfumes that our kids had given her over the years." Travis fanned out his hand as if he was showing an expansive array. "She'd just squirreled it all away. Jewelry that I'd given her and the kids had given her." He pursed his lips. "All never worn."

Rhett offered his uncle a sad smile. Aunt Pearl had been one of his favorite people growing up and he knew, despite her stubborn streak, Travis missed her every day. Letting the man talk would do no harm.

"Pearl grew up poor, you see," Uncle Travis said. "I don't know whether she was waiting for a time she deemed special enough to use those things, or if she just didn't believe *she* was special enough to use them. But in the end it didn't matter, did it? All those things, those pretty things, all of them went to waste. Unused. Rotting and tarnished or full of dust. Pearl never got to enjoy them because she didn't believe she was worth enjoying them."

Rhett looped a hand around the back of his neck and rocked in his boots. "Why are you telling me this?"

"Like I said——" Travis's voice was wistful "——a gift is only as good as what you do with it." His uncle tugged on his suit jacket and made his way toward the door. "Remember, son. 'For unto whomsoever much is given, of him shall be much required.'"

It had been a while since Rhett had cracked the book. "I know the Bible, Uncle Travis."

He paused as he opened the door. "Ah, but do you know the heart of God in this matter? Have you sought *that* out, son? Because that's more valuable than a hundred memorized Bible verses." Uncle Travis shrugged. "Just a thought."

After his uncle left, Rhett fought the urge to sit back down and drop his head into his hands. Fought the desire to finally lose it over his dad's death. Fall apart once and for all. But he couldn't do that, not now. Maybe not ever.

Way too many people were counting on him to be strong.

Rhett mentally packed up every messy emotion in his heart and shoved them into a lockbox. He pretended he was jamming them down, squishing them until they were so small and insignificant they weren't worth thinking about. Or talking about or sharing with anyone.

No one would care about them anyway.

Then he clicked the lockbox shut and tucked it into the darkest corner of his mind to be forgotten.

Macy was going to pace a hole in the floorboards at the front of the ranch's office. Travis Jarrett had left half an hour ago, but Rhett still hadn't vacated his father's office. What was taking so long?

She jerked her hair up into a ponytail.

The second—the very second—he left that office he'd have to listen to her, hear her out.

She'd *make* him.

Macy paused near her desk and picked up a framed photo of her and Brock Jarrett. It had been taken at last year's spring kickoff event for Camp Firefly—the free summer camp

Brock ran at Red Dog Ranch for foster kids. She traced a finger over the photo—Brock's smile.

Macy blinked away tears.

After her father walked out of her life when she was ten years old, Brock had stepped in and filled that void. And when her mom died eight years later the Jarretts had moved her onto their property. Rhett's dad had been family to her—*Rhett* had been like family to her too. Now they hardly acknowledged each other, and with Rhett's mom fading fast, Macy couldn't help but feel like she was losing everyone she cared about all over again.

"I'll keep your secret," she whispered to the image. "I promise."

She set the picture down and absently rubbed her thumb back and forth across the raised scar on her pointer finger. A nervous habit she'd tried, unsuccessfully, to break more than once. The scar was Rhett's fault. Six years ago, he had dropped his cell phone when they were out hiking and she'd crawled back over the large rocks on the trail to get it, disturbing a copperhead in her zest. Of course, Rhett had carried her to safety, rushed her to the hospital as her skin swelled and blistered and the pain intensified, and stayed by her side while she healed. The memory caused a rueful smile to tug at her lips. He had lost his cell phone after everything anyway.

She forced her thumb to stop moving.

The scar on her finger wasn't the only one she blamed him for. The Do Not Cross tape coiled around her heart was all his doing too.

Macy whirled toward the door to Brock's— no, Rhett's—office.

Enough.

She marched toward the door and didn't bother knocking before opening it. "We need to—" The words died on her lips. Rhett wasn't there.

The man must have slunk out the never-used back door like the guilty dog he was.

Macy balled her fists.

They would have to face each other—have to talk at some point—and today was as good a day as any. She hadn't been able to get a good read on Rhett with Travis there so she had held her tongue.

I'm looking into cancelling programs.

Not if Macy had anything to do with it.

She grabbed her keys, locked up the office and hoofed it out into the yard. Orange mingled with pink and gold in the sky. A slight breeze carried the chill whisper of the approaching night. The sun had dipped close to the horizon, not quite sunset yet but soon enough.

Various structures peppered the Jarrett property. The office and main buildings serving the summer camp wrapped through the front of their land, including ten camper cabins and a mess hall that was built into the side of the largest hill they owned. The barns and cattle fields took up the opposite end of their holding, and the family home rested like a gorgeous crown jewel at the end of the long driveway. Macy lived in one of the small bungalows tucked just west of the family ranch house. A handful of staff members lived on the property.

Macy passed the small corral that housed Romeo, the ranch's attention-needy miniature donkey, and Sheep, an all-white miniature horse that belonged to Rhett's niece, Piper. Romeo trotted beside the fence line as she walked, trying to coax an ear scratch out of her.

"Not now, buddy." Macy didn't break her stride. Still, his pathetic bray made her heart twist. She loved the little donkey and all of his quirks—maybe *for* his quirks. "I'll bring you apples later, deal?"

Beyond their enclosure, she spotted a horse and rider picking their way through the bluebonnets blanketing the nearby field. She squinted, trying to focus on the rider. Shannon Jarrett, Rhett's sister. Despite the fact that none of the women were related, Shannon, Cassidy and Macy had formed a tight-knit sisterhood. Especially during the last five years.

Macy climbed onto the fence and waved at her friend.

Shannon nudged her horse into a trot so she was within yelling distance in seconds.

"Did you see where your rat of a brother went off to?" Macy called.

Shannon tossed back her head and laughed. "Well, I know you aren't talking about Boone." And neither mentioned the other Jarrett brother, Wade. His death five years ago had been the catalyst that set the Jarretts drifting apart. Being Wade's twin, Shannon had been deeply affected by the sudden loss of him. She hadn't quite regained the wide, carefree grin she'd been known for as a child. Probably never would.

"I could hardly call a man training to be a pastor a rat." Macy joined in the laughter.

Shannon nodded, her short blond waves bobbing. "Rhett walks Kodiak to the lake every morning and every evening. I don't think she can last a day without swimming. Rhett says it's in her breed's blood."

Macy tipped her head in a silent thank-you and made for the lake.

Red Dog Ranch sat on over three thousand acres of gorgeous Texas Hill Country land and had multiple lakes and ponds. Some of them Macy would need a horse or one of the trucks to reach, but she guessed Rhett had stuck to the one closest to the house. Long ago, she and Rhett had dubbed the body of water Canoe Landing. It was where he'd fished with his dad and where he and his siblings had learned to swim. Macy too.

Embers of memories burned in the back of her mind. She snuffed them out. A million yesterdays couldn't help her solve the problems she faced today.

When Macy hiked over the hill that led to Canoe Landing, she paused. Rhett had his back to her. His shoulders made an impressive cut against the approaching sunset. Rhett had always been taller and broader than his brothers. The Wranglers and starched button-down he wore fit so well, they might as well be illegal. Under his cowboy hat she knew his hair would be naturally blond-tipped and tousled.

He was the kind of handsome that female

country-western singers wrote ballads about, but it was clear he had never caught on to how attractive he was or how many hearts he could have broken if he'd wanted to. Rhett wasn't like that.

She fiddled with the end of her flannel.

Kodiak bounded out of the water, dropped a soggy ball at Rhett's feet and then leaned around his leg and let out a low growl. Her yellowish eyes pinned on Macy.

Rhett pivoted to see what had captured his dog's attention. His eyebrows rose when he spotted Macy. His eyes were such a shocking shade of blue and his tanned skin only made them stand out more.

I'm sorry I kissed you and ran off.

I'm sorry I never returned your calls. I was confused. I let too much time pass.

I ruined everything.

She swallowed the words rushing through her mind.

Macy tucked her thumb over her scarred finger. "You snuck out the back?"

Rhett patted Kodiak's head before he lobbed the ball in a wide arc. It splashed down in the middle of the lake. The dog became a blur of brown along the shoreline. She dove into the water, going under before paddling wildly.

Rhett crossed his arms over his chest. "I didn't know I was supposed to check in with the assistant before leaving."

"Listen." Macy squared her shoulders and lifted her chin a notch higher to hold his gaze. "We need to come to some sort of a truce here or else work is going to become very miserable, very fast."

Unless he fired her, of course. Rhett had the power and ability to do it, so while she wanted to push him and fight with him over the foster-related events at the ranch, she needed to tread the subject carefully.

Good thing Macy had cooled down considerably since she'd locked up at the office.

Rhett shifted his line of vision to watch Kodiak swimming in circles. "I suppose you're right." He glanced back at her. "We can't keep acting like the walls of Jericho to each other if we're going to be sharing office space."

"You're...you're going to let me stay then?"

The notch in Rhett's throat bobbed. His gaze traced her face. "This is your home, Mace. You love your job." He looked away. "I don't plan on taking that from you."

"Thank you," she whispered. She tentatively touched his arm. "Rhett, I'm so sorry about your dad. He loved you a lot."

His bicep tensed under her touch. " I thought we had plenty of years left. I never thought—" A harsh exhale of breath escaped his lips. "What a stupid thing to say. No one expects these sorts of things."

"I'm here." She squeezed his arm lightly, then let go. "If you need someone."

His brow bunched as his eyes cut back to her. "We haven't spoken in three years."

"The walls of Jericho fell down." Macy slipped her hands into her pockets. "You know that, right?"

A muscle in Rhett's jaw popped, once, twice. "I'm a… I'm not looking for friendship again, Mace. Not with you. I think it's important to put that out on the table."

She knew Rhett hadn't meant the words maliciously; he was just stating reality. Rhett was a man who dealt in facts. It was his attempt at being forthright. Chivalrous even, making certain no one would get the wrong idea from the get-go.

But, wow, what he said smarted.

Not with you.

Those three words stung her worse than any pit viper ever could.

After Brock's funeral she'd foolishly hoped she and Rhett might have been able to let bygones be bygones and fall back into the easy, lifelong friendship they had once shared. A part of her had even wondered if God was drawing them close for another chance at being together in the way Macy had always wanted.

Well, consider that balloon popped and tossed in the garbage.

"Understood." She kept her voice even. If they weren't going to deal in niceties she might as well get down to business. "We need to talk about the foster programs."

Rhett let out one sharp laugh that held no hint of humor. "Which one?"

"Let's start with Camp Firefly." As if summoned by her mention, a pack of fireflies began to flit over the lake. Kodiak had noticed them too and began snapping her giant muzzle in their direction. The little bugs looped and pitched in oblong circles around each other. Encouraged by their presence Macy said, "You can't cut it."

Rhett cocked his head. "Who said I was?"

"You did." She jabbed a finger in his direction. "Mr. I'm-Looking-into-Cancelling-Things."

Rhett rubbed his finger across his lips. Was he hiding a smile? Was this a *joke* to him?

Kodiak slogged out of the water. She gave

a shake, sending droplets flying, and then walked toward her master, her tail wagging the whole way.

"I can't make any promises about next summer, but with only three months left until camp it would be hard to cut it." Kodiak dropped down at his feet. She adjusted to lay her head near his boots, leaving wet marks on the legs of his jeans. "Some of the kids have already gotten letters inviting them. No matter what you think of me, I'm not heartless, Macy." He cut his gaze to collide with hers. "I promise, I'm not."

"I know you're not," she whispered into the growing dark. Rhett had never been a spiteful person. Hurt, but never hurtful.

They both stared out over the water as the sun tucked itself further into tomorrow.

"It's just…" Macy looked up into the sky as if she could find the right words somewhere in the clouds. "Your dad really cared about these programs. He cared about each and every foster kid. I'd hate to see *any* of the programs get cut."

Rhett stiffened. "My dad cared more about those foster kids than he did about his own flesh and blood." There was no trace of a smile left on his features. Only hurt mixed with a hint of disappointment. "You know I'm right."

Bringing up Brock had been a mistake, but it had easily slipped out. Brock and Rhett's relationship had been tense since Wade's death. They'd fought over blame instead of helping each other grieve. Macy had never understood how the fault of a boat capsizing in the Gulf of Mexico could belong to either of them.

Rhett tapped his thigh, causing Kodiak to rise and follow after him.

"Rhett, please," she said. "The foster programs, they're important. They were started because—" Because of you, she almost said. *Right or wrong, they were supposed to be Brock's love letter to you.* "There has to be a way to make it all work."

"It's late. Mace. We can talk about it tomorrow." He tipped his hat and walked past her up the hill in the direction of the Jarrett house.

Macy stared after him, watching Kodiak's tail bob in rhythm with Rhett's footfall—the whole time wanting to call after him, wanting to spill her secret so he could understand once and for all. So she could help him work through the hurt he felt over his father.

But she could never tell Rhett that he'd once been one of those children in need.

That Brock and Leah Jarrett had adopted him.

Chapter Two

When Rhett padded into the kitchen at the family ranch the next morning, Shannon offered him a cup of coffee with a sad smile.

He declined. Shannon consumed at least six cups of the stuff a day, but Rhett had never taken to it. That hardly stopped his sister from trying to get him to drink it whenever she could.

However, he wished he was a coffee drinker because it had been a long night.

Rhett bit back a yawn. "Does Mom walk the halls yelling like that often?"

Shannon nodded, swiping at her eyes. Then she took a long swig from her mug.

Guilt stabbed through Rhett's chest. Strong and palpable.

For the last three years he'd been gone, running Straight Arrow Retrievers, his dog-training business more than a hundred miles away from Red Dog Ranch. For his mom's sake, Rhett had made a shaky truce with his dad and had visited the ranch a few weekends a year. It had been difficult to find days to visit when Macy wasn't going to be on property or he would have visited more often. Foolish now that he thought about all he had missed. All for stubborn pride. He had missed his mother's decline, missed so many days when he could have been spending time with her. Rhett rubbed his jaw.

He had kept in touch with Shannon, Cassidy and Piper with phone calls and video chats and they had often made the trip out his way for visits when he hadn't been able to come home.

But he hadn't been around when his mom had started showing symptoms. Hadn't gone along to the countless doctor appointments. Hadn't been a part of the discussion when her plan of care was decided. And having only been back living in the family house for three days, Rhett scarcely knew how to speak to his mother any longer.

Dementia.

Such a small word for such a life-altering disease.

Before now the extent of his knowledge had

sadly been gleaned from TV ads that rattled off more about the dangers of the marketed drug than actually showing the truth of the illness. Commercials that depicted smiling elderly people watching their grandchildren play or sitting hand in hand with their equally elderly spouse.

All lies.

Rhett hadn't been at Red Dog Ranch to watch his mom's mind deteriorate, but Shannon had. Boone had too, up until he had enrolled in a divinity school last year, moving his wife and daughter out of state in the process.

Rhett opened his mouth to say something to Shannon but closed it just as quickly. What was there to say? "I'm sorry" sounded small. Too little, too late.

Six months ago Brock had hired a nurse to be with Mom during the day while he was working and he managed her care at night, but now with Brock gone...they needed to figure something out. Rhett made a mental note to pull out his mom's insurance information and check over the plan to see what it would cover. The day nurse always arrived before breakfast every morning, but Rhett needed to look into the possibility of having someone with her at night, as well.

Ever present, Kodiak followed him to the fridge.

"Not much in there," Shannon offered. "You'd do better to head to the mess hall. Cassidy does most of the staff meals there." She jerked her chin to indicate the direction of the mess hall. It was located where the biggest hills began to roll through their property. Their father had insisted on building the dining hall there so that a huge, long basement could be constructed into the hill. All the nonperishable bulk food used to cook staff meals and feed the kids who came for summer camp could be stored there in a cooler environment without wasting tons of energy. The concrete basement also served as a great spot to find momentary relief from the heat of summer. Brock had searched for a contractor who would build into the shape of the land like that for a long time. Basements were rare in Texas.

His mom shuffled into the room, her hand resting on her nurse's arm. Rhett had seen plenty of his parents' wedding photos and snapshots of their dating history to know that his mother had always been a beautiful woman and maybe even a touch regal in how she carried herself. Now in her midsixties, he thought she looked a bit like the actress Helen Mirren. Outwardly she appeared healthy, but her pale blue eyes told the real story…she looked through him vacantly. She smiled pleasantly at him, almost blandly, as the red-haired nurse helped her into her chair.

A large common room made up the heart of their home. Vaulted ceilings with exposed beams gave the house a grand bearing, and a stone fireplace in the sitting room only added to that feeling. Every stone had been mined from Jarrett-held land. The kitchen flowed directly into a dining room and the large sitting area. In the sitting area, the wall without the fireplace boasted two-story-high floor-to-ceiling windows. From Mom's vantage point, she could gaze out to the wide lake where he took Kodiak for her swims and beyond into a field of bluebonnets.

Her chair looked as if it was about to swallow her petite frame. As she gazed around the room, her eyes never really landed on anything in particular. It struck Rhett that she looked lost.

Lost and scared.

His throat felt as if someone had stuffed a

bale of hay down it, followed by some of the pebbles that made up the driveway. Rhett swallowed hard, once, twice, three times before he could get any words out. "How are you this morning?"

She pursed her lips. "Do you know where Brock is? I've looked everywhere but, by the cat's yarn, I can't find him."

Rhett glanced at Shannon, who gave an infinitesimal shake of her head. *Don't tell her. Don't correct her about Dad. Don't correct her at all.* Shannon had gone over the rules with him in regard to how to deal with Mom a handful of times in the days since he'd been back. But every time Mom asked... Well, someone might as well have kicked him in the stomach while wearing steel-toed boots. And then sucker-punched him in the jaw for good measure afterward.

Their mom had been present at the wake and funeral. She'd wept with Boone and Rhett each on either side of her, holding her up. She *knew*.

But right now, she didn't. Her mind was living in the safer Land of Before.

He wouldn't lie to his mother, but he'd learned quickly there was no reason to cause her undue emotional trauma either.

Rhett cleared his throat. "I haven't seen him in some time."

True. Far too true.

His mother dipped her head. With shaking fingers she traced a swirling pattern into the armrest of her oversized chair. "He's probably off somewhere with Wade, don't you think? It feels like forever since I saw my baby boy."

Shannon's coffee mug clattered against the kitchen island's stone countertop. She braced a hand on the counter and the other was pressed against her heart. "She mentions him—" her whispered voice broke "—all the time. I can't..." Her shoulders trembled as she hurried out of the kitchen.

Rhett wanted to go after her, but what comfort could he really offer? The family had lost Wade when he was only nineteen years old. Nothing he would say to his sister could change the truth of what had occurred. Wade was gone and Rhett couldn't make the anguish of losing her twin disappear.

Grief over Wade threatened to swallow Rhett in equal measure to what he felt over losing his father. Wade had stormed off spewing hurtful words at the whole family the day Rhett had cornered him, confronting Wade about every horrible thing Wade was involved in.

You know what? Don't worry. You'll never have to see my pathetic face again. Wade's final words came back to bite Rhett. His brother had left the ranch and headed straight for the Gulf of Mexico and boarded a small party boat. When the boat capsized everyone on board had been too intoxicated to get off in time, to radio for help.

Wade had been right. They never got to see his face again.

Brock had blamed Rhett for Wade's death. Rhett shouldn't have spoken to his brother that way. Wade would still be with them if Rhett hadn't confronted him. But Rhett had shot back that it was Brock's fault for allowing Wade to flounder for so long, allowing him to go down a wrong path years before he drowned. For investing more into the nonprofit at the ranch than his own son.

Rhett and his dad had never completely patched the bridge between them after that. Rhett walking away from the ranch had only solidified the tension in the relationship. If given the chance, Rhett would have handled both Wade and his father differently.

There were things Rhett would take back if he could.

So many things.

But right now he could only move forward. Do better. Be present.

Rhett shifted from one foot to the other. "I believe you're right, Mom, about Wade and Dad being together." His voice caught on the last word and he prayed she wouldn't notice.

She folded her hands in her lap and looked toward the lake. "Just as I thought. Still…" Her voice trailed off for a heartbeat. "I'm looking forward to when Wade comes back. I long for the day you and him are in the same room together again."

"Mom," Rhett said, keeping his voice even. "Wade may never come home."

"Don't you say something so horrible." His mom met his gaze. "He will. My boy will."

Before he left the house Rhett pressed a kiss to his mom's forehead, made sure she didn't need anything else and checked in with the nurse, Louisa. He should have headed straight to the mess hall, but his boots pointed south of there, in the direction of the little white chapel his father had built soon after he started Camp Firefly.

Rhett checked his phone. He was so used to having it on silent because the ring tones and even the vibrate setting interfered with training dogs. Most of them he trained using whistles and other noises so distractions were unwelcome. He had texts from a few of his clients who had been in the middle of sessions when his dad had passed so he'd put them on hold. They'd been patient, but training built week by week and he needed to either continue with them or send them to a new trainer, or else the dogs would lose their momentum.

Rhett made a split-second decision—offering them time slots if they were willing to come out to the ranch and refunding them if they didn't want to drive so far. One client texted back immediately, confirming a time slot for the next day. They were eager because they already had their dog signed up for contests. Two more asked for refunds and referrals to other trainers.

As he approached the church, he noticed that someone had used large white stones to outline a path leading to the chapel's front door. It was set up on the hill nearest to the mess hall. A wide cross had been erected on the hill years before the chapel's creation. At the end of each camp session, his father had the kids write on rocks the last night and lay them at the foot of the cross—usually a word symbolizing something they were trusting God for.

Distantly, he wondered if they'd kept up that

practice after the church had been built. Would he have to lead that ceremony this summer?

Rhett tested the door. Open. He slipped inside, slid off his hat and stooped to dodge the end of the bell rope. Sunlight streamed through the stained-glass windows, painting the dull brown carpeting with a brilliant prism of colors.

Do you know the heart of God in this matter? Have you sought that out, son?

Of course he hadn't. If he sought out what God wanted...it wasn't worth it. If the Bible was true—and Rhett believed it was—God seemed to ask for dangerous, impossible things. Rhett was trying so hard to keep himself together, he couldn't afford dangerous faith right now.

Rhett gripped the edge of a pew. He hadn't willingly set foot inside a church in five years. Not since learning about Wade's death. His father's funeral had been held in a church, but he didn't count that time. He had entered that church out of duty, not choice.

If Rhett's own father—his flesh and blood— hadn't cared enough to know about his dreams and worries, he couldn't imagine God would either. Much like Brock had been, God was busy with far more important things than Rhett and his heart. After all, God had a universe to run. Rhett's small slice of the world hardly measured up to that. And he couldn't blame God for not concerning Himself with what must be Rhett's miniscule burdens in the very grand scale of human history. But it sure made Rhett want to keep his distance.

Rhett considered himself a Christian, but he certainly didn't like to bother God.

"You may not care about me, and that's fine." A wash of embarrassment flooded through Rhett at the idea of talking out loud, but he pressed on. "But Shannon... Please... could You be there for Shannon? She's been through a lot and I don't know how to help her. And Mom, God, please. It's hard. Seeing her that way."

The weight of so many new responsibilities sagged onto his shoulders. His father's death hadn't only made the ranch his obligation, but in a very real way Rhett had become the head of the Jarrett family. A role he wasn't sure he was cut out for. Between worrying over what his mother needed and his concerns for Shannon, he already felt stretched thin.

And then there was Macy. Macy touching his arm by the lake last night. Macy saying she was there if he needed her. Macy studying him with those large brown eyes that seemed to know everything about him. Rhett swallowed hard. Working alongside her was going to be difficult because the truth was, he missed his friend.

But he couldn't forget that he'd offered her a job at his business and when she'd showed up on his doorstep it was to turn him down, to pick the ranch—to pick his dad—over being near him. Worse, when he had tried to usher her inside so they could talk things over she had grabbed his shirt and kissed him—a kiss he had never known he had wanted until that point but afterward had never been able to get out of his head.

Then Macy had run off.

Rhett had left messages for two weeks. Messages she hadn't returned.

Now he had to see her every day and it was hard to forget their old friendship, the jokes they had shared over the years. That kiss.

Kodiak whimpered behind him.

Attempting to alleviate the tightness building in his chest, he blew out a long stream of air.

It didn't help.

Macy wrapped her fingers around the mug in her hands and prayed she wasn't making a huge mistake.

From the wide bank of windows in the mess hall, she had watched Rhett veer off the walkway and head toward the chapel. Witnessed him duck inside. The minutes had ticked by and curiosity had gotten the better of her.

Patience might be a virtue, but it was one that Macy sorely lacked.

Now in front of the chapel, she rested her hand on the doorknob and sucked in a fortifying breath.

Rhett did not want her friendship—he'd made that crystal clear last night—but coworkers should be civil to each other. An employee could check and see how her boss was doing without it meaning friendship, right?

Besides, she knew him too well to ignore the fact that he was obviously under a lot of stress. Her heart went out to him. If only she could convince him to share his burdens. He didn't have to manage everything alone. He wasn't alone at all.

She opened the door and let it close with a thump behind her so as not to startle him with her presence. He swiveled around in his seat. His hair was sticking out in adorable angles, reminding her of old times when he'd been a sleepy, hopeful boy swapping secrets with her around the campfire instead of the serious man he'd grown into. An awful twinge of longing stirred through her. She missed the Rhett who had been all dreams and optimism. He had changed once he hit high school, closing up a little more with each football game his father failed to show up to. Each broken promise.

But his hair wasn't sleep mussed. The particular style he was sporting at the moment had been caused by him grabbing the tips of his hair and yanking as he thought through something. She'd seen him do it enough times to recognize the signs.

"I can leave." He rose and put his hat on. Ever beside him, the large dog stood when he did. "It's all yours."

She held her free hand up in a stop motion. "I came to see you."

His left eyebrow arched.

"Here." She extended the mug and walked down the aisle. "A peace offering."

"What are we making peace for?"

"Last night at the lake."

His large dog edged to sit a few inches in front of the toes of his boots as if the beast was concerned that Macy might try some ninja-attack move on Rhett at any second. As far as

Macy could tell, the animal had appointed it-self as Rhett's personal guard.

As if a man with muscles like Rhett needed one.

"Is that thing safe?" Macy looked down at the dog.

He nodded. "She won't do anything unless I tell her to."

She handed Rhett the mug. "Earl Grey Crème black."

His features immediately softened and he cocked his head as he accepted the mug. "You remembered my favorite tea?"

"Your favorite *drink*," she corrected. Un-like most of the cowboys and staff at Red Dog Ranch, Rhett had never taken to coffee. After she'd tried the Earl Grey Crème black tea that he preferred, she had to admit it was delicious. It was a perfect balance of milk, sugar, vanilla and bergamot flavors while still delivering a welcome kick of caffeine.

My dad cared more about those foster kids than he did about his own flesh and blood.

Regret formed a lump in her throat. She glanced at the light bleeding through the stained glass windows, then glanced back at Rhett. "I'm sorry. Last night when I brought up the foster programs and your dad… I know that still hurts."

He blew out a long stream of air, looked away. Nodded to accept her apology.

A part of Macy wanted to tell Rhett that Brock had loved him and the rest of his family. Maybe Brock had been bad at showing it, but they had been his life. His passion for foster kids had bloomed from his love of family—he'd wanted to give kids without homes the same opportunities and security that his children had been afforded.

But right now wasn't the time.

With Brock gone, it might never be the right time.

Macy searched for a way to connect with Rhett, anything that could encourage conversation. She needed to establish easy communication between the two of them so they could work alongside each other for the best of the ranch. And if she was being honest, her heart squeezed at the sight of her oldest friend looking so…lost. Despite what he had said last night, she wanted to connect—wanted him to know he wasn't alone.

Her gaze landed on his dog. *Perfect.*

"So, when did you acquire your ever-present

shadow?" She smiled, hoping he could see the words were kindly meant.

"Kodiak." The dog perked up when he said her name. It was a good name for her because the dog's coat was the same red-brown color of a Kodiak bear. Her fur went slightly curly near her neck and back haunches.

Rhett grinned down at Kodiak and stroked behind her ears. "She was a training failure." His voice was warm. "Weren't you, girl?"

"She looks well trained to me."

His smile dimmed when he looked away from Kodiak to meet Macy's gaze. "What I mean is, her owner brought her to me to be trained and then she bonded to me and refused to go back with her owner." He crossed his arms over his chest. "It's not generally seen as a good thing."

"Well, she seems happy with the arrangement," Macy said.

"Her breed is extremely loyal." Kodiak let out a groan, protesting at the absence of his pets. "So once they pick their person it's an almost impossible bond to sever." He relented and tapped his fingertips on her head. "The breed can be hardheaded."

"Her breed?"

"She's a Chessie." He must have noticed Macy's confusion. "Sorry, that's dogspeak for a Chesapeake Bay retriever. People hear the retriever part and think they'll be like Labs or goldens, who love everyone and everything, but Chessies aren't like that. They're affectionate with their family but are extremely protective and don't warm to strangers easily."

As if to demonstrate what Rhett was talking about, Kodiak butted her head against Rhett's knee but kept her yellow eyes trained on Macy the whole time. The dog was definitely suspicious of her.

Macy inched back a half step. "Does that happen a lot? Training failure?"

"Thankfully, she was my only one. But her owner was my first client when I started the business so failing on the first one..." He rubbed his chin. "Well, let's just say that was like a bull kick to the ego. I almost thought about turning tail and coming home." He cleared his throat. "Back here, I mean."

She'd never known he considered returning to Red Dog Ranch.

"Rhett, that last time we saw each other..." Macy said.

When I kissed you.

Rhett held up a hand. "We're different peo-

ple than we were three years ago, Mace. I don't
see the point of backtracking down that road."

When her boyfriend had broken up with her,
she'd driven the hundred miles. She'd shown
up on Rhett's doorstep. He had thought she
was there about the job he'd offered her, but
she had grabbed his shirt and yanked him into
a kiss. She would never be able to forget how
his body had gone rigid. He hadn't returned
the kiss and, when she broke away quickly, his
eyes had been wide, horrified. "Why did you
do that?" he'd asked. Repeated it twice.

And she had turned around and run back to
her car. Too mortified to face him for months
afterward. It had been the action of a woman
who had read a man wrong.

So completely wrong.

Rhett had never cared for her. Not like that.

Not like she'd wanted him to.

Macy rubbed her thumb over the jagged scar
on her pointer finger. "Why didn't you come
back home? After Kodiak, I mean?"

He lifted his shoulder in a half shrug. "There
was nothing to come back to."

*I'm not looking for friendship again, Mace.
Not with you.*

Macy tugged her inner shield closer in an
attempt to make his words bounce off of her

harmlessly, but they went around her defenses and struck the tender places left in her heart. She'd thought she had walled off the part of her that cared about Rhett—about all men—because she knew there were no romantic relationships waiting in her future. Not now, not ever. If Rhett, who had known her better than anyone in the world, could see her completely and find her lacking...could not want her... then no one would.

No one wanted Macy Howell. Not for the long haul. Not her father, not the ex-boyfriend who had started the fight between her and Rhett three years ago and not her closest friend.

Why didn't anyone ever fight to be with her? What made her not worth it?

Because something's wrong with you.

Hot shame poured through her body.

Macy took another step back and fought the warring desires to slam her finger into Rhett's chest as she gave him a piece of her mind or to turn and run so she could go lick her wounds in private. But if she wanted to help the foster kids, she couldn't do either. She needed to be able to work with him, talk to him.

Relax. This isn't personal. It will never be personal again.

She forced a long drag of air through her nose.

Macy might not matter to anyone, but she could make her life matter by fighting for the kids. By making sure Rhett didn't end up cutting the programs they all looked forward to.

She let a breath rattle out of her. "Kodiak's a good fit here." *There, back to a safe topic.* Macy gestured toward Kodiak. "Red dog. She could be the ranch's mascot."

Rhett frowned. "She's brown."

Macy narrowed her eyes, pretending to examine Kodiak. "It's definitely a reddish brown." She wrapped her fingers over her opposite elbow.

Kodiak looked up at Rhett with such adoration.

"You were always fond of dogs," Macy said. "I guess training them was a given."

"Dogs make sense." He shrugged. "You don't have to be anyone special to gain their loyalty. A dog is simple to figure out. They only ask for kindness and time spent together."

"And treats."

He smiled. "And treats."

She hugged her stomach as she watched him walk out of the chapel, her mind roiling with so many emotions it was difficult to sort through them. But one thing was certain: it was going to be near impossible not to fall for Rhett Jarrett all over again.

Chapter Three

Kodiak snored near Rhett's chair as he sifted through the files Macy had left in his office yesterday. Each name and picture made his heart twist.

Gabe Coalfield, seventeen, wants to be a veterinarian someday.

Harris Oaks, eighteen, would be happy to do anything to have a job.

Deena Rich, seventeen, just wants to feel useful for once.

Rhett pushed the papers away and covered them with one of the financial ledgers. As he made decisions he wanted to continue being able to think of all the children involved in terms of a faceless, nameless group—not as individuals with hearts and dreams.

With ambitions in their lives he might crush if he closed the ranch's doors to them.

He pinched the bridge of his nose.

Why had he been put in this situation?

Going over the calculations in his father's books had only solidified Rhett's decision to cut programs. Brock had neglected the cattle business that went along with the ranch, among other things. While the Jarretts enjoyed the cushion of an ample bank account for now and healthy investments in a few other areas, the ranch hadn't turned a profit in years, which meant Brock had been slowly dipping into the family's savings in order to keep the daily functions of the ranch running.

Fine to do once in a while, but the records showed it had become the way of Red Dog Ranch. That couldn't stand any longer. If they kept operating in such a manner, eventually funds would run out. Money Rhett needed to pay for his mom's medical care. Funds he needed to use to compensate staff dependent on the ranch for their livelihoods.

Additionally, he wanted to be able to leave Wade's daughter, Piper, and Boone's daughter, Hailey, something someday. As well as any other nieces and nephews who might come into the family down the road.

His father may not have cared about the Jarrett legacy—about providing for the long-term future of their flesh and blood—but Rhett did.

And there was nothing wrong with that.

Rhett dug his elbows into the desktop and sat straighter in his chair.

He would not allow himself to feel guilty for doing the right thing.

One of the teenager's photos had slipped loose when he shuffled them under the ledgers. Rhett picked it up and studied it. The girl had crooked teeth; her smile appeared forced. The look in her eyes—lonely and beaten by life—gutted him. She would have an internship, but she represented so many kids waiting for an opportunity, a break. One he was considering taking away.

He turned the picture over.

A soft knock on his door. Macy, more than likely.

Rhett massaged his temples. Earlier in the chapel he had opened up way too much to Macy. How did she do that to him? They'd been around each other for twenty-four hours and his resolve to stay distant had already crumbled.

And she lived a stone's throw from his house, so even when they weren't in the office he couldn't escape her presence. They hadn't spoken in three years and yet she *knew* him. Knew how his mind worked. Knew how he ticked. It was unnerving.

He dropped his hands to his desk and studied the spot on his arm where her fingertips had rested.

Since they were little, Macy had always had a way of cutting through his nonsense and zeroing in on pieces of Rhett he thought he'd hidden from the world. Then again, he'd always been terrible at playing hide-and-seek.

When they were young, it had been one of Macy's favorite games. She'd never failed to find him and find him quickly. However, she had also possessed a knack for unearthing the most unimaginable spots to hide in. Once they were a little older it had become near impossible to ever locate her. Most times she ended up having to reveal her spot, no matter how hard he'd searched.

It would seem he was still terrible at hiding from her.

"Come in."

She opened the door, clipboard in hand. Her smile was tentative. "Have you had a chance to go over the files I left?"

He nodded.

She took the chair on the other side of his desk. "Great. Let's decide who each of them will be placed with."

"Do you know what a liability it is having them here? Our insurance rates are sky-high with all the minors on the property." He had spent a chunk of his morning reading legal nonsense and now his head felt foggy with all the information.

"The social workers have signed off on the waivers," she reminded him.

Rhett sighed and slid the files to her side of the desk. "You can go ahead and make all the placement decisions. You've been at the ranch all this time and I'm only just back, so I'm deferring to your knowledge here on what's the best fit for each of them."

She didn't move to pick up the paperwork. Macy opened her mouth. Closed it. Looked toward his mom's painting and then back at him. "I'm more than happy to help." She spoke each word deliberately. "But your dad always wanted to be a part of the process. He said it was—"

"Mace," he cut in. "If you haven't noticed by now, I'm not my dad."

"I realize that. I should have phrased that differently." She hugged her clipboard to her chest. "No one is asking you to be a replica of Brock."

Wasn't that *exactly* what everyone wanted him to be? His dad's will had set him on a lifelong course where he'd have to hear again and again and again how he didn't measure up to Brock. If he succeeded with the ranch he'd have to hear how he was following in his dad's steps, and if he failed he'd have to hear how disappointed his dad would have been.

"Aren't they?" He hated how hoarse his voice sounded.

She offered him the hint of a smile. Her wide brown eyes studied his face. "I'm not."

Wasn't she though? After all, wasn't she the one who kept bringing up how his dad had done things?

"I really promise I'm not." She gave a small shrug. "It's just really hard to strike him from all conversations when I'm missing him."

Understandable. Talking about Brock was clearly healing for her, but the same thing opened Rhett's wounds deeper.

"Then what do you want, Mace?" His question was soft, guarded. "Because when you look at me like that…"

She skewed her lips to the side as if trying

to find the right words. "I'm just wondering where the boy I knew went."

He sighed. She might as well have said she didn't like the person he'd become.

Not that it mattered. He shouldn't care about what an old friend thought of him.

Rhett crossed his arms. "He grew up."

"That's a pity," Macy said. "He had this amazing ability to dream big but plan well, stay rooted and focused—something this place really needs. He had the heart and determination to grow Red Dog Ranch into an amazing place if he'd wanted to. I think that boy could have shaped the ranch into something beyond what his father possibly ever could have."

He clenched his teeth and reminded himself that Macy was just being Macy. She'd been known to kick a hornets' nest before—literally. She'd treat him no differently. It was her nature to push and he had loved that about her.

Just…not right now.

He pressed his palms against his armrests. "You finished?"

"For now, sure. Forever?" she asked. "Not a chance."

Rhett couldn't hold in the chuckle that escaped from his lips, though it had an edge of desperation in it. "I don't doubt it one bit."

This was the Macy he remembered—his Macy—someone who would stand against the wind and glare at a coming storm. Someone who didn't flinch.

Well, not *his* Macy. He wasn't quite sure where that thought had come from.

Macy ran a slender finger down the to-do list on her clipboard. "Now, about the Easter egg hunt…"

"Wait. That's still on?" He flipped through a stack of paperwork in his dad's inbox. "I'm sorry, I'm not caught up on everything. I thought we still had time to alter things." And he had figured his father was waiting until the last minute to reach out to previous vendors like he always had. His father had possessed a huge heart, but he hadn't been much of a planner. Rhett had been considering his father's lack of planning a blessing for once because it would make the event easier to cancel if nothing had been set in stone yet.

Her eyebrows shot up. "Of course it's still on."

Rhett rubbed his forehead. "How much do we usually spend on it? In total."

She thumbed through a few pages on her clipboard. "At least ten thousand. We always have a huge turnout," she added quickly.

Some people might have thought she was estimating high, but Rhett didn't believe she was. The Red Dog Ranch Hunt had become an event that drew many foster families from far away. People booked every room at nearby hotels in order to attend. The event had taken on a life of its own, complete with his father hiring a private helicopter pilot to drop candy over the fields as the children watched. When it came to these events his father had been nothing if not excessive. They also provided a full ham supper for around a hundred people who stayed afterward. The dinner was a ticketed event that raised money specifically for a college scholarship program for foster kids. Not to mention purchasing the eggs and prizes, paying staff to run various games and do setup, hiring a company to put up and tear down decorations and seating. Renting outhouses and paying for random other items.

Honestly, she was probably guessing low.

Rhett flipped the ledger to the latest financial records and twisted the book in Macy's direction. "Tell me how we can afford to host any event with this kind of bank account?"

Macy sucked in a sharp breath. "I had no idea he'd let it get this bad." She held up a finger. "He would sometimes mention that we should cut expenses here and there and then never did it so I figured we were fine. I never pushed the issue."

"Seriously?" He cocked an eyebrow. How could she not know? She'd been his assistant.

Macy waggled her head. "I promise you, I had no idea. You know how your dad could be about these things. He managed the accounts himself. I entered the bills into the finance software and entered payroll, but I only handled submitting those expenditures for his approval. I didn't balance the accounts. I never *saw* the actual money in the account." She pulled the ledgers closer. "Oh, Rhett. What a mess."

He believed Macy. Brock had been a man who kept many things close to his chest. Judging by how she had responded, Rhett knew she had never seen these books. Hadn't realized the foster programs were draining the family's personal accounts.

Rhett pressed his fingers against his forehead. "My dad had a big heart."

She looked like she might cry. "He had a *huge* heart, but that doesn't excuse this." She gestured toward the ledgers.

Rhett nodded. "Huge heart. Not a lick of business sense."

Macy snaked her hand across the desk to cover his. "You have a better sense for these sorts of things than he ever had." She gave his hand a pump.

Rhett slipped his hand from under hers and it instantly felt cold, lacking. He could have so easily turned it over and leached comfort from her, but he had to keep his head on his shoulders when it came to Macy. Uncle Travis was right. Macy could help him—but Rhett had to stay focused on keeping their partnership about working toward what was best for the business.

"So you understand why we have to nix the egg hunt this year?" Rhett asked. "Can you double check the recent bills to see if the ranch has made any deposits to secure vendors? I doubt it, but a quick check can't hurt." His dad had been notorious about scrambling at the last minute to get things done. Rhett tucked the ledger away. "That's potentially thousands of dollars we can immediately save."

Macy held up a hand. "I think recouping as much as we can is the right step. But, Rhett, we can't outright cancel the egg hunt." She tugged a newspaper clipping from her stack of papers and shoved it toward him. "It's already run in the paper."

Of course his dad would set up the announcement while procrastinating on the actual work of pulling together the hunt.

Instead he groaned. The sound made Kodiak's ears twitch. "This is bad."

Macy set down her clipboard. "What if we can run the event without touching your family's money? Or at least, minimally touching it. We can do this. We just have to think it through."

"I don't see how that's possible."

"If we work together, I think we can secure donations and get others to pitch in. I'll look through the bills and see if we can get refunds on the few things he might have secured, and if not refunds maybe we can renegotiate the contract terms." Her eyes lighted with excitement. He could practically see the wheels turning in her head. "If we can do this without too much expense, are you on board?"

"I'm tempted to say yes." Rhett was worried it would be hard to throw an event together so quickly, but his dad had done it all the time. Besides, Rhett knew not to doubt Macy's tenacity. "Though it will be a lot of work in a short amount of time."

"We've faced bigger obstacles together," she

said. Macy sent him an excited smile. "I don't doubt what we can accomplish if we both commit to this."

He couldn't say no. Not to that smile. "All right, then. Let's do this."

"Great." She popped up. "In that case, I've got a lot of work to do so I'm going to dive in right away." She reached to grab the clipboard she'd forgotten in her exuberance. "We can do this."

He gave her a thumbs-up.

When she was about to leave, Macy hesitated in the doorway, her back to him. "You know, you don't have to be your father." She slowly turned to face him, her hand braced on the frame. "But you do need to be the best Rhett you can be. You need to live up to the potential God's placed inside you." She moved her hand from the frame so she could hug her clipboard to her chest. "Understood?"

Standing there with her chin held high, her eyes slightly narrowed at him and pure challenge lighting her features... Rhett had never seen anyone more beautiful.

The realization forced all the oxygen from his lungs.

"Mace, I—" His voice cracked.

"I'm going to be here, beside you in this." She pointed at him. "And I'm going to keep challenging you."

That's what he was afraid of.

In the following days, Macy tossed herself into researching how to plan a charity event and began to make a list of all the companies and local residents she could call. She made a second list that she dubbed her pie-in-the-sky list that was made up of actors, famous singers, news anchors at the big stations, radio deejays—anyone she believed was worth reaching out to. Even if one or two of them chose to give a monetary donation, it could make a huge difference. Texas was home to plenty of celebrities and many of them were proud to support Texas-based events.

Hey, a person could dream.

It was something she'd learned from Rhett when they were young. Too bad he'd lost his wide-eyed belief in chasing after big dreams somewhere along the way. Though his dog-training business had been a bit of a dream chase for him, hadn't it? Maybe there was still a part of the boy she knew somewhere inside the jaded man. Deep, deep inside.

Macy found herself praying while she worked—often more for Rhett than anyone else.

Please help me help him. Give me the right things to say when we interact. I know he's hurting and he probably hasn't talked about it to anyone.

A boy with freckles and a wide grin ducked his head into her office. "Hey there, Miss Howell."

She rose from her desk and smiled at the teenage boy. Gabe had attended Camp Firefly for the past four summers and he volunteered hours at the ranch, mucking stalls and helping feed the horses, already. Making him an official intern had been a no-brainer.

The interns were starting today.

Rhett was working with one of his dog-training clients in the far field again, so they had agreed that she would give the kids a quick tour and then hand them off to their appointed mentors to shadow for the day. Macy was happy Rhett had started seeing his clients again and wanted to do whatever she could to encourage him to keep his business alive. It had only been two appointments so far, but she knew he loved training dogs and didn't want him to have to lose Straight Arrow Retrievers.

Initially Macy had challenged Rhett about working with the foster kids, but she had promised herself she would stop forcing Rhett to do things the way his father had. Just because Brock had insisted on training the interns himself, it didn't mean Rhett had to. With that in mind, she had told him she would help run things—help take the load—so it was nice to see he was willing to trust her to do just that.

Macy joined Gabe outside and introduced herself to the seven other interns. She rattled off the speech she'd heard Brock recite multiple times but knew she wasn't doing it justice. Normally Brock spent the first two or three days showing the interns the entire ranch and explaining every part of its workings. He introduced them to every staff member and made sure they knew what to do in an emergency. He got to know them and made sure each one felt valued at the ranch. But with plans for the egg hunt looming over her, each day—each hour— was an imperative for Macy to seek donations and coordinate every aspect of the event. She also had to start devoting time to mapping out the plans for Camp Firefly because summer would be here before they knew it.

So for the first time in the history of Red Dog Ranch, Macy handed the interns over to each of their appointed mentors right after the tour and headed back to her office. She worked on drafting letters to some of the people on her second list—the dream-big list—and emailed them before her nerve waned.

Less than an hour later, Gabe banged open her door. He was panting and his face was tomato red. "There's been an accident. Miss Howell, you've got to come quick!"

Macy sprang from her desk. "What type of accident?"

Gabe was already at the front door, motioning frantically. When he saw she was following he headed out the door and started running for the closest horse enclosure. "This way."

Judson, one of the ranch's field hands who had been assigned to be Gabe's mentor, was crouched over Piper, Rhett's four-year-old niece. Piper was curled in a ball sobbing, her tiny shoulders shaking.

Rhett came tearing across the opposite field, Kodiak at his heels. Rhett's face drained of color as he dropped to his knees beside Piper and lightly brushed her long brown hair from her forehead. "What's wrong, sweetheart?"

His chest heaved. No doubt Judson had radi-oed him and Rhett had sprinted the whole way.

Kodiak whimpered as she pranced around the pair.

"M-m-my aarrrrm," Piper wailed.

It was then that Macy noticed Piper's arm was twisted at the wrong angle. Broken. Ma-cy's stomach threatened to pitch.

And suddenly, as she watched him crouch over Piper, Macy noticed the back of Rhett's neck turn red. "How did this happen?"

"Uncle Rrrrhett. It hu-hurts." Piper's whole body shook. "Huurrrts." Kodiak crawled for-ward and gave Piper a tentative lick on her cheek.

Macy hadn't noticed Judson take off when they appeared, but he must have headed for the barn. He came back, sprinting in their direc-tion with one of the red emergency totes full of medical supplies that were stowed all over the ranch.

Judson panted. "I called Cassidy. She was in town getting groceries but she's on her way back. She should be here in minutes."

Wordlessly, Rhett took the medical bag and found the sling inside. Since Piper was so small, he knotted the top to shorten it. Then he helped her sit up.

"I'm so sorry, baby girl. This might hurt."
He gingerly lifted her broken arm and set it in
the sling. She let out a yelp of pain and started
to cry harder, her cheeks going red.

Rhett pressed a quick kiss to the top of her
head. "You're so brave. That will help your
arm not move around too much until the doctor can see it."

She bit her trembling lip and nodded. Despite him living far away for much of her life,
Uncle Rhett was her favorite person in the
world and it was obvious that she trusted him
completely. He'd given her Sheep, the miniature horse, for her birthday and her mom, Cassidy, had often talked about the weekly video
chats Piper and Rhett had when he lived far
away.

Cassidy's van rounded down the driveway.

Rhett scooped his niece into his arms, avoiding the injured arm.

He turned toward Macy. "Find out what happened and call me."

He gave both Judson and Gabe a significant
look. Then he charged toward the van with
Piper in his arms. Seconds later they watched
Rhett, Cassidy and Piper head off toward the
hospital.

Macy prayed that Piper would be okay and

that nothing else was wrong with her, and she prayed for Rhett too. The man was fiercely protective when it came to his family and he was bound to want consequences for whoever had let Piper get hurt.

Thirty minutes later, once Macy had calmed down an upset Gabe and a profusely apologetic Judson, she called Rhett. She'd already texted with Cassidy, but she knew she needed to talk to the boss. "How's Piper?"

"Broken arm and a sprained foot." He sounded tired. "She says the kid put her on one of the big horses bareback. Is that true?"

Macy sagged into the chair at her desk. "Judson went into the barn for a minute. He knows he shouldn't have left Gabe on his own with one of the horses, but we know Gabe well. He mucks the stalls for us all the time." Macy pressed on.

"Piper knows Gabe so she ran out to see him. Gabe said Piper told him she wanted to ride the big horse so he let her sit up there. He turned his back for a second." The teenage boy had been so upset about the little girl getting hurt. He had teared up in Macy's office. "He didn't realize the horse was only green broke. He thought it was one of our calm trail horses. He didn't know, Rhett. He's just a kid himself."

When Rhett didn't say anything, she continued, "Judson was going to teach him how to work the green broke correctly, so he went to get a longer lead line. That's the only reason Gabe was out there alone." She was rambling, but Rhett had to understand that it was an accident, pure and simple. "It could have happened to any of us."

"And if Piper had said she wanted to light the mess hall on fire—" Rhett's words were clipped "—would he have let her do that too?"

Macy dropped an elbow onto her desk and pressed her forehead into her hand. "This wasn't his fault."

"So is it Judson's?"

"It was an accident, Rhett. Accidents happen." She knew it wasn't wise to get into this on the phone, but Macy had always had a hard time biting back her words. Frustration was hard to pack away for later. While Rhett lived by facts, she was fueled by emotions.

"An *accident* took my brother. An *accident* took my dad. I'm done with accidents, Mace."

Ouch. He was right. But facing losses, facing accidents, didn't mean a person should never take a risk again. "Next time—"

"There won't be a next time. Our intern program ends today."

That immediately cooled her thoughts. "You don't mean that."

"I already sent messages to all the teens."

"Rhett, please. Just hear me out," she said. "The intern program doesn't cost the ranch a cent, but it provides free labor. It makes zero sense to cut it when we're trying to save money."

"If a kid other than my niece gets hurt and someone sues us, how's that saving money? Or if an intern got hurt? Managing interns divides the staff's focus. It's really not as mutually beneficial as you might think."

"Rhett—"

"I'll talk to you later, Mace." And he was gone.

Couldn't he understand that even with a mentor nearby things could happen? People got hurt every day. It was called life. Piper was a perfect mix of curious and courageous, which meant she was always taking risks. Rhett wouldn't be able to protect his niece from every bump and bruise in life no matter how hard he tried.

He loved his family fiercely. It was a quality Macy had always found attractive about him, but she found herself wishing he cared about the foster kids too. Maybe it was wrong to put that on him—he wasn't Brock and she didn't want him to be Brock. Really she didn't.

But she was so torn between the family she loved and the children she was dedicated to helping. Macy needed to decide where her loyalties lay. With the man who had once stolen her heart? Or the kids who desperately needed an advocate?

If only the answer could be both.

Chapter Four

Rhett entered the kitchen section of the mess hall where he knew he'd find Cassidy and Piper. It had been a few days since the accident, but he still wanted to make a point of checking on his niece first thing each morning. Guilt clung to his shoulders as he spotted Piper in her cast. If Rhett hadn't been in the far field with all his attention on the dog he was training, he might have prevented her injury.

It confirmed what he had feared all along. He would never be able to run the ranch, the family's charitable foster programs and Straight Arrow Retrievers at the same time. Not well. Not successfully.

Something had to give.

And unless he could find a loophole in the

will, it was clear which of the three he would have to let go.

"How's my little soldier holding up?"

Piper rounded one of the wide metal islands in the industrial kitchen. Her hair was back in her normal braided pigtails. She had on jeans, tiny boots and a button-down shirt speckled with pink flowers. "I am *not* a soldier."

The little pout she wore reminded Rhett of Wade so much it made his chest ache. He would do anything to take care of these two ladies—for the brother he had lost. The brother who might still have been around if Rhett hadn't pushed him away.

Rhett cleared his throat.

"Tell him, Mom." She spun toward Cassidy.

Cassidy used the back of her hand to shove light red hair away from her eyes. "It's cowgirl or nothing, Uncle Rhett. You know better."

Rhett dipped his head. "Of course. My mistake. How's our little cowgirl holding up then?"

Piper straightened her spine and held her head higher. "I'm not *that* little anymore."

He bit back his smile. At four years old, Piper barely came above his knees. She took after her mother, petite for her age. Wade had also been the shortest of all the Jarrett siblings.

But what Piper lacked in height she made up for in personality tenfold.

Rhett narrowed his eyes, making a show of examining her. "Now that you say it, you do look taller today."

Cassidy hid a grin as she filled a metal pancake dispenser with batter. It looked like a large funnel, but when she pressed the handle it released the perfect amount of batter onto the huge skillet, making it easy to dish out hundreds of pancakes in very little time.

At least, Cassidy made it look easy, but then she had always had a knack for cooking even at a young age. Rhett was sure he would make a mess of everything if he tried to use the contraption. Set him in a pen with five growling dogs? No problem. Ask him to fix breakfast for a crew of thirty workers? Not a chance. Cassidy was the expert here.

Fresh pancake batter sizzled as it cooked. Glass containers full of maple syrup rattled in a pan of boiling water on the nearby stove, permeating the air with their overly sweet scent.

Piper pushed away the sleeve on her right arm, revealing her hot-pink cast. "Look at how many people signed it." She grinned at him as she tapped an inch of blank pink. "I'm saving this spot for Gabe though."

Rhett lightly set his hand on her head. "Gabe isn't going to be back at the ranch, honey."

Her eyebrows went down. "How come?"

Cassidy glanced over her shoulder from her spot near the griddle. "You didn't make him leave because of what happened, did you?" She went back to flipping pancakes, moving the done ones onto a large platter. "Rhett?" she dragged out his name.

The hum of people talking in the mess hall told him that the staff was starting to pile in for breakfast. No time for long explanations. Even if there had been time, he wouldn't have the talk in front of Piper.

Rhett pushed his fingertips against the cool metal of the island. "She got hurt because of him."

And because of me.

Piper tapped on his leg. "He didn't push me."

"I know, but—"

"So it's not his fault." Piper folded her arms and locked onto him with a hard stare. Had she been taking lessons from Macy? All Rhett knew was he was steadily losing to a four-year-old.

"But—"

"Accidents happen." She looked toward Cassidy. "Right, Mom?"

Cassidy directed the kindest, most loving smile at her daughter. "Sometimes an accident can turn out to be the best thing that ever happened to us."

Rhett knew she was talking about becoming pregnant with Piper when she was only eighteen. About the gift that was his niece—a piece of his brother that lived on even though Wade was lost to them. But surely Cassidy hadn't forgotten that Wade had died in an accident of all things.

"Sweetheart." Cassidy motioned toward Piper. "Can you go put the butter on the tables?"

"I can even do it with my cast. It doesn't stop me. Nothing stops me." Piper collected two small plates from the counter and headed into the mess hall. She was used to helping her mom in little ways, especially with the morning meal.

Rhett shoved his hands into his pockets. "She's a lot like her mom."

"Flattery isn't going to get you out of this talk," Cassidy said.

He waited until Piper was long out of earshot before responding, "The fact is most accidents have consequences. Bad ones."

"Don't you think I know that? After what

I've been through? Come on, Rhett." Cassidy scooped the last of the pancakes onto the wide platter. "I want Gabe to still have a chance." She passed a platter to Rhett. Her rule had always been every person taking up space in the kitchen had to help. Looked like Rhett would be serving the food at the meal. When she picked up the second platter he reached to take it from her.

She didn't let go right away. "He needed the internship. The boy wants to be a veterinarian and those schools are hard to get into. Scholarships are even harder to come by. He needs to be able to put us on his résumé. If he can show he interned with the animals here, it'll give him a better chance at succeeding. Remember being like that? Like him? Needing a start?"

Of course he remembered. Rhett had been that boy not that long ago.

Chest deflated, he broke eye contact. "I already cancelled the program."

She let go of the platter and folded her arms. "Then uncancel it."

"I can't."

"Being the boss around here you're the one person who can do just that." She sighed, unfurled her arms and dusted her fingers off on her apron. "Everyone deserves a second chance, Rhett. Everyone."

"What if I can't manage the program adequately?"

"Then accept some help." She pinned him with a stern look. "No, I'm not talking about hiring people. Even though you refuse to acknowledge it, you have a huge support system here. So many people willing to help you. But I think you have to learn to be willing to accept help first."

He wasn't really sure he understood what she was getting at and he told her so.

"You know how I said everyone needs a second chance?" Cassidy arched an eyebrow. "Well, that includes forgiveness. Sometimes I think you're holding yourself back for something you think you did wrong. Some sort of penance that maybe you don't even realize you're forcing on yourself. I wish you would forgive yourself for whatever you think you did. You deserve a good life, Rhett. Don't be burdened by something you're forcing yourself to carry, okay?"

Rhett swallowed hard. Cassidy had always been a straight shooter.

"Promise me you'll think about it," she said.

He nodded. "I will."

"But not for too long." She pointed a spatula at him. "You Jarretts can be the worst type of overthinkers."

This time he didn't fight the smile. "I would love to say you were wrong."

"But you know I'm not." Her voice was an odd mix of hope and disappointment all in one. There was more on her mind than their current conversation.

She shooed him toward the door leading out to the mess hall. "Now get breakfast out there before it goes cold."

"Will do, sis."

He knew she was right about people needing second chances. Although, if it was up to her, sweet-spirited Cassidy would give everyone in the world a tenth and eleventh chance. Everyone would have unlimited opportunities to turn their life around for good. But having a sympathetic nature had gotten her into trouble in the past.

He couldn't afford to make the same mistake.

The fact was, Piper's injury rested heavily on his shoulders. The accident wasn't Gabe's fault. No, Rhett was to blame. He had thought he could set aside his responsibilities at the ranch for a few hours a day to continue working with clients. He had been wrong.

Macy finger combed her hair as she rushed up the steps to the mess hall. She shoved through the front doors to discover the dining area empty save for the cloying smell of maple syrup and bacon lingering in the air. She'd missed the staff meal completely but perhaps Cassidy had some leftovers tucked away.

Cassidy stuck her head through the wide serving window that connected the kitchen to the eating area. "If you're looking for Rhett he left down the back stairs a few minutes ago. Said he was making a call. He might still be down there."

"Rhett?"

"Tall, handsome guy." Cassidy held a hand in the air demonstrating how tall he was. "Partial to dogs and cowboy hats. Runs the place," she teased.

"Huh." Macy played along. "You mean the one stubborn as sunbaked cowhide?"

Cassidy winked. "Same guy."

"Not here for him." Macy splayed a hand on her stomach as she entered the kitchen area. "I'm here for food."

"Tough break." Cassidy wiped down one of the metal islands. "I'm fresh out of pancakes."

"That's terrible news." Macy wasn't exaggerating. She had a soft spot for breakfast foods and Cassidy was an excellent cook. Cassidy's pancakes deserved sonnets written about their greatness. "I overslept."

Cassidy stilled. "You?"

"I know." Macy held up a hand in defense. "I was up late working on details for the Easter egg hunt."

"How about this? You come in here and help me with dishes and I'll whip up a batch of chocolate-chip pancakes just for you." Cassidy motioned toward the wash area. "We can talk while we work."

Macy wasted no time rolling up her sleeves and heading to the deep sinks. She fished the scrubber out of the warm water and went to work on the first pan she found. "When I suggested to Rhett that we could plan the egg hunt without using much money, I might have bitten off more than I could chew," Macy confessed. "I've been racking my brain trying to think of businesses we could approach as sponsors and I could ask them, but I know they would be more willing to donate if the pitch was coming from Rhett, you know? Everyone always dealt directly with Brock."

Cassidy carried a few more dirty dishes over to where Macy was stationed and plunked them into the sudsy water. She paused nearby. "So why don't you go and ask him to do just that?"

Cassidy had always been so matter-of-fact about things and Macy appreciated that character trait. Though not a Jarrett by blood, Cassidy was very much a part of their family—more so even than Macy, who had spent her whole life with the Jarretts. Macy's mom and Mrs. Jarrett had been friends since high school, so Macy had been visiting Red Dog Ranch since she was one week old. Where there had been cracks and brokenness in Macy's family, she had seen what she thought was perfection in the Jarretts. They were kind, they loved each other, they spent time together.

Despite everything, she would never be connected to the Jarrett family in the way Cassidy was. Never connected in the way she had always wanted to be. Accepted, but not one of them.

Suds splashed onto Macy's shirt as she forcefully scrubbed a pan. "Rhett has a lot on his plate right now. Besides, I'd love to demonstrate that I can take care of something like this on my own—prove that he can trust me."

"First, refusing help doesn't necessarily mean capable." Cassidy pursed her lips. "Second, Rhett already trusts you completely."

Macy knew Cassidy had a soft spot for Rhett. When the family had finally accepted Wade was gone, Rhett had been the one to track Cassidy down and offer her a place at Red Dog Ranch. Her parents hadn't been supportive of her keeping her baby—they told her doing so would ruin her life. But Rhett had convinced her that she was as good as family to the Jarretts and she and her child would always have a place here. He had been the protective older brother Cassidy had never had.

Macy sighed. "He trusted me at one point in life, but that was a long time ago."

"All right. That's it." Cassidy tapped a finger on the counter. "Out with it, already."

"What—"

"Don't play coy with me," Cassidy said. "It's time you shared what went down between the two of you—because all I know is that one day you two were thick as thieves and then he left the ranch and you two suddenly started avoiding each other. It's boggled my mind for the last three years and I'm never going to get a peep out of Rhett, so you're going to have to be the one to spill."

He didn't want me. I made a fool out of myself.

Macy blew dark strands of hair from her face. "What's there to say? We grew apart."

"Oh, don't feed me that line." Cassidy shook her head. "You won't get out of this that easily." She tossed a dirty dish towel into a laundry basket they kept near the sink. "We're friends, aren't we?"

Macy pulled the plug from the sink, letting the water drain away. "Of course we are."

"Then tell me the truth."

"I want to." Macy trailed her thumb over the scar on her pointer finger. "I just don't think you understand how hard it is."

"Here's what I do understand. If I could turn back the clock to when Wade and I had our last fight—" Cassidy's voice clogged with emotion "—I would have done anything to stop him. To go after him. To get him to come home. *Anything.*"

Macy wiped off her hands, making sure they were dry, and then rubbed Cassidy's back. "I know you'd do anything to have Wade back. Wade loved you. I know he did. But what happened between Rhett and me…it's not the same."

Cassidy turned so her hazel gaze connected with Macy's. "You have a chance to make things right between the two of you," she whispered. "A second chance, Macy. Don't squander it. I'd give anything to have that with Wade."

Macy wrapped her arms around her stomach. "Did Rhett ever tell you he offered me a job? He wanted me to leave the ranch with him. Move away. Not together, of course." Macy flushed, hoping Cassidy didn't get the wrong impression. "He offered a high enough salary to cover rent in the area and things like that. An option so I wouldn't be dependent on Red Dog Ranch for a home."

Cassidy popped up so she was seated on the counter. "He never said a word. I'm assuming you said no."

Macy nodded. "I did, but… I went to turn him down in person. Remember I was dating Jim? He broke up with me. Over Rhett. He accused me of being in love with Rhett and not him, and I'm ashamed to admit he was right."

"I honestly don't know why Jim held on for so long. Anyone with eyes knew where your heart was." Cassidy batted her hand. "And we don't need to feel bad for Jim. He's happily married and all that jazz now, so it's all a good ending for him."

"I drove to Rhett's new place right from the breakup and thought about how much I cared about Rhett the whole way there. When he opened the door... I don't know what came over me." Macy wrung her hands and looked away. "I literally clenched my hands in his shirt and yanked him down for a kiss."

Cassidy pumped a fist in the air. "You know it, girl!"

Macy covered her face with her hands. "He froze. He didn't kiss me back."

"He was probably just taken by surprise," Cassidy offered.

Macy swallowed hard. "When I stopped he said 'Why did you do that?' all horrified. He said it a couple times."

"What did you say?"

"Nothing," Macy said. "I turned and ran back to my car."

"Oh, no."

"Oh, yes." Macy shrugged. "He called and left messages for the next few weeks saying he wanted to talk, that—" she put her fingers up to make air quotes "—we needed to discuss what had happened." She lowered her

hands. "But I was mortified. I avoided him."
After a lifetime of rejection from her father,
then the breakup with Jim, which she realized
was right but had still hurt, Macy hadn't been
able to face Rhett's rejection maturely. If she
could turn back the clock she would handle it
all differently, but turning back the clock only
ever happened in children's bedtime stories.
"By the time I decided to swallow my pride
five months had come and gone. I called him
once, all those months after. He never called
me back. And that was it."

Cassidy arched an eyebrow. "You two have
talked about this since though, haven't you?"

"It was three years ago." Macy repeated
what Rhett had said. No matter how much she
wanted to make things right, if Rhett wasn't
willing to talk there was nothing she could do
about it. "Everything's changed now. It's not
worth rehashing."

"Macy." Cassidy hopped off the counter and
took her hand. "That man loves you. He always has."

"Yeah." Macy released a long stream of air.
"Like a brother."

"You're wrong and I know you don't believe me." Cassidy offered a sad smile. "But

I loved one of the Jarrett boys. I know how they think."

Macy needed to steer the conversation away from anything that would make Cassidy think of Wade. "It's later than I thought. Can I take you up on the pancakes another day?"

Cassidy nodded. "You never responded to my text —are you coming to our girls' movie night tomorrow night? Shannon picked out *To Catch a Thief.* Come on, you can't say no to a Cary Grant movie."

"You know me too well," Macy said. "Of course I'll be there."

Cassidy gave her a thumbs-up and then headed toward the back room. She paused when she reached the threshold. "You should talk to him, you know."

"I'm actually going to track down the man in question now." Not that she was going to talk to him about their awkward moment three years ago, but she didn't need to get into a circular argument with Cassidy over it.

Macy checked her watch.

She also had an appointment to keep in town and an idea simmered at the back of her mind. If she could convince Rhett to go along, maybe, just maybe the meeting could be the first step of his softening toward the ranch's mission as far as foster kids were concerned.

Lord, please help me convince him.

"I think he's still downstairs." Cassidy jutted her chin toward the stairwell located along the side of the kitchen which led to the basement area. "I never heard the door open down there. It's heavy and makes a loud sound whenever it closes."

Macy nodded and headed toward the stairs. She knew about the loud door and hadn't heard it slam either. She paused at the top of the steps. When Cassidy was out of sight, Macy tugged out her phone and typed in Straight Arrow Retrievers. Macy had never gone to his website or sought out information about his business because doing so would have been like tearing open stitches for her emotionally. She had avoided all mentions of Rhett in order to protect her heart. If she could pack him away she wouldn't have to hurt.

But he was here now.

She might as well know.

Listing after listing popped up, revealing articles written about the awards that dogs he'd trained had won. One about a dog who now starred on a television show. Another dog he'd trained was being considered for induction into the Master National Hall of Fame—one of the highest honors a hunting dog could obtain.

"Oh, Rhett," she whispered. Her throat felt thick with both pride and sadness. He had accomplished so much in such a short amount of time. And while he had scheduled a few training appointments at the ranch, how much had he truly sacrificed in order to return home and meet the terms of the will so his family could keep the property?

The low timbre of his voice drifted up the stairs. From where she stood, she couldn't make out his words, but she was happy she wouldn't have to go out searching for him.

How many hours had she and Rhett spent as teens, and even into their twenties, hanging out in the mess hall's basement? They had often run to the basement for their breaks during the summer and fall working hours in order to escape the heat and sun outside. Built into the hillside, the large basement area stayed cool even on the hottest day. They used to sit on the pallets, knee brushing knee, and talk about everything.

She pushed cherished memories away. They only hurt. What was the point of reliving memories when she had no hope of ever making more with her old friend?

Macy tucked her phone into her back pocket, rolled her shoulder and took a deep breath as she headed down the stairs.

Chapter Five

Rhett huddled on a pallet in between a stack of industrial-sized cans of tomato sauce and boxed pasta. He stared at his phone's screen, willing his friend Hank to return the voice mail he had just left. He had discovered he got surprisingly good cell reception in the basement the other day, no doubt because a neighbor rented out land to a company to place a cell tower on his property.

For a second Rhett considered joining Kodiak outside. After he had seen to her breakfast, Rhett had left her basking in the sun by the door that led outside from the basement with a bowl of water nearby. But as peculiar as it sounded, something about the cement walls and low ceiling brought Rhett comfort. Made him remember easier times.

The edges of the long basement were lined with pallets balanced on cinderblocks, a way to keep the non-perishable food stored in a cool area away from the floor. The back end of the basement curved, providing a nook at the end that was great for hiding. Even with all the splendor outdoors, this had always been one of Rhett's favorite spots on the property. He and Macy had called the back wall home base. If they'd needed to meet or got split up while working or during a game, this was where they'd always found each other later. Their meeting spot.

Something he hadn't thought about in a long time.

Something he probably shouldn't think about.

Still, an image from their talk in his office flashed to mind. Macy with her head held high and a spark of pure stubbornness lighting her face. In that moment, she had taken his breath away and he couldn't get it out of his thoughts. Since then ideas kept pestering him. Why hadn't he come to terms with his feelings for her sooner? That day when she'd kissed him, it had been an unexpected—albeit not unpleasant—shock. Never good about surprises, he had reacted poorly. His mind had started overthinking, making his body freeze...pretty much the worst thing he could have done in the situation.

If he could do it all over again? He would have wrapped his arms around her and he would have kissed her soundly, senselessly. Then he would have begged her to never leave his side.

But he had botched his chance at happiness with Macy. She had called him after the kiss, once. It had been five months after everything had happened, but Rhett had been bitter about her ignoring all his initial calls five months before. He hadn't returned her call, figuring it was her turn to try calling for weeks without an answer. But she had never called again. He always wished he had just swallowed his pride and returned her call.

His life could have been so different if he hadn't been petty in that moment.

A part of him wanted to reinstate their friendship. He missed having her as his closest confidant. But when she had tried to broach the subject he had shot it down, if only to not have to hear her say they should disregard what happened and go back to being friends. The fact was he didn't want only friendship with her and never would. He *couldn't* only be her friend.

But what about the very small chance that she wanted that too?

No. He had to stop that train of thought. Rhett didn't have time for a relationship with Macy or anyone. If he ever entered into a relationship, he would want it to be at a time in his life when he could give his partner the attention she deserved, which was definitely not now.

Not that he wanted one. He was fine alone. Great, even.

He scrubbed his hand down his face.

In another part of the basement they stored extra bedsheet sets and items staff or guests to the ranch might need. His father had wanted to meet basic needs for anyone staying on their property and never wanted any of the kids to feel embarrassed or ashamed if they didn't have necessities required for overnight stays.

It was something Rhett might not have thought about. Scratch the *might*—he certainly wouldn't have come up with keeping toothbrushes and new stuffed animals on hand. His mind simply didn't work that way. Yet another reminder he had no right attempting to run the foster programs at the ranch. Even if he could right the boat in a financial sense, he would never do Camp Firefly or any of the other programs justice. He lacked so many traits that had been second nature to his dad.

Rhett dropped his head into his hands.

He needed to let go of the grudge he harbored against the foster programs and the kids involved. It wasn't their fault his dad had chosen them over his son. Rhett wanted to let go of his resentment. Truly. But how does someone cut out a piece of their heart that's hurt for thirty years? What would be left if he did let it all go?

Maybe he shouldn't have sent the will to Hank. Maybe the only way to get over his grudge would be to forge ahead, embracing all the foster programs. But they couldn't feasibly keep it up without affecting the long-term security of his family's finances. What a mess. If only he could separate the hurt his father had inflicted from how he felt about the programs.

He stared at the phone again. Should he call Uncle Travis? He closed his eyes. His uncle would tell him to make his dad proud or utter something along those lines. Give Rhett a one-way ticket for a guilt trip he hardly needed, considering he was already good at taking that trip on his own time.

His phone vibrated. Hank.

Rhett answered immediately. "Thanks for calling me back. Were you able to review the files I sent?"

Hank chuckled. "Well, hello to you too, buddy."

"Sorry. It's just—"

"Kidding with you, Rhett. Lighten up."

Rhett used his free hand to rub at a kink on the back of his neck. "Words one rarely hears from a lawyer."

"Oh, now, we're not all bad. You wouldn't be calling me if you thought we were."

"True." Rhett had trained Hank's German shorthaired pointer, Riptide, who had gone on to title in the American Kennel Club's National Hunt Test. After Riptide's training was complete, Hank and Rhett had remained in touch, becoming friends. Being an intellectual property lawyer, Hank had assisted Rhett with trademarking his business.

"I will say—" Hank blew out a long breath "—that's one hefty will."

"I really appreciate you taking the time to look at it for me."

"No problem."

"I haven't had any guidance on it," Rhett confessed. "My family doesn't understand the risks involved." He paused but when Hank didn't jump in Rhett kept speaking. "Tell me you found a loophole in it. There's a way to get out of the part about the extra programs if I need an out, right? I would think the part about serving foster children could be inter-preted in different ways." Rhett knew he was rambling but he couldn't help it. Uncle Travis had said the terms of the will were very clear: Red Dog Ranch had to continue being used to serve foster children or Rhett lost the inheritance—meaning his family would lose their home.

The floor above him creaked, making him glance upward. The beams supporting the kitchen and mess hall floors had to hold quite a bit of weight. All the machinery and sometimes hundreds of people. If something broke—how much would it cost to fix any issues? Even re-placing pieces of flooring and subfloor here and there added up. The camper cabins all needed work before the camp session, as well. The horse barn had some long-standing issues he needed to address. Maintenance was a con-stant. More money. More needs.

Rhett's chest felt tight.

"If I need to prove the financial burden or whatever it takes, I can certainly do that."

The fingers on Rhett's free hand had fisted, resting on his knee. He deliberately uncurled each finger. *Relax*.

"Slow down." Hank spoke in a calm tone Rhett had heard him use before when he was in lawyer mode. "I looked over everything and at first glance it seems fairly binding. However, as you know, this isn't my wheelhouse."

Rhett's gaze bored into the gray cement wall opposite him. How had that comforted him minutes ago? Now it reminded him of a cell. Trapped. Cold. Alone. "So you don't think there's a way out for me?"

"Now, I didn't say that."

"Then what are you saying?"

"I'm saying lawyers know lawyers. I have a friend from college—he specializes in estate law," Hank said. "I haven't spoken to him in a few years, but let me reach out to him and see if he's willing to take a look at it for us. I can't promise you anything but I'm certainly willing to try."

"I owe you." Rhett asked about Riptide and Hank promised to call if he heard back from his friend. Rhett shoved his phone into his back pocket and rose. He was too tall to stand straight in the basement so he had to crouch somewhat. It was time to get on with his day.

He rounded the corner and came toe-to-toe with Macy. His boots shuffled back a step. Loud and clumsy on the floor.

Macy's dark hair hung over her shoulder, free of its usual ponytail, and Rhett couldn't help but stare. Other than at his father's funeral, lately she had worn it up. Even under the dim basement lights it had a shine to it, like a raven's wing in the sun. Rhett had the odd desire to tuck her hair behind her ear just to know what it felt like.

Instead, he shoved both hands into his pockets.

When he finally met her gaze her left eye twitched.

Rhett's mind raced back through his talk with Hank. How much of his conversation had she overheard? He swallowed, trying to find words. Why was he having a hard time speaking?

But all she said was, "Found you."

Rhett forced his shoulders to relax. "You always could."

She cocked her head and studied him for the space of a few heartbeats. "Physically, yes."

He scuffed his boot on the floor, a nervous habit. All the long days, all the years spent with Macy, and he had never been flustered around her.

He cleared his throat. "Remember when we used to play hide-and-seek all the time?"

"I do. You never could find me." She crossed her arms over her chest.

He sighed. "I guess you were just too good at hiding."

She shrugged, but he knew her too well to miss the tense set of her shoulders and her inability to maintain eye contact for more than a few seconds. Macy was keeping something from him.

"Maybe you should have looked harder," she said.

They weren't talking about a child's game anymore, were they? Was it foolish to hope she was talking about their kiss? About what might have happened between them? Rhett hedged with, "Next time, I will."

The barest hint of something that looked as if it wanted to be a smile played across her features.

Moving on.

"How long have you been standing there?" Had she pieced together he was enlisting legal help to outsmart his father's will? If she had,

Rhett expected her to be furious. But Macy didn't look upset. Maybe a little confused.

Her brows furrowed. "I was hoping I could convince you to drive into town with me."

He rubbed at the back of his neck. She hadn't answered his question. "There are calls I have to make and I need to check the pole barn and do you know we still haven't hired a veterinarian since Lyle retired?"

Tentatively, she touched his forearm. "Those things will all be waiting for you this afternoon. I promise. We could split up those calls. Divide and tackle together."

"I don't know." Had Macy missed him as badly as he'd missed her that first year? How many times had she picked up her phone to call him, finger hovering over his contact? Because he'd done so daily for longer than he would ever admit. He had grieved their friendship.

Grieved what could have been if only he had realized he loved her sooner.

But she had been fine, hadn't she? Happy here with the people and place she had chosen.

She hadn't mourned their friendship. At least, that's what he told himself.

All Rhett knew was after the kiss he'd called her at least twenty times and she had called him once during the three years.

Once.

Letting her in—even for a morning together to do errands—was a risk Rhett wasn't sure he was willing to take. Then again, what could it hurt? It might help if he could get a better sense of her—understand her passion for the foster programs and maybe see them in a light other than what it had done to his relationship with his father.

"Trust me," she said. "Take a leap and trust me on this."

Curiosity made his resolve waver. He crossed his arms. "Persistent much?"

"You know it." Macy tugged keys from her pocket. "We're going into town to secure donations for the egg hunt. When we decided to go forward with the event you agreed we'd do this together, remember?"

"I did, didn't I?" And there went his resolve completely.

She popped a hand onto her hip. "I'm not taking no for an answer."

"Now that right there. That's the Macy I know." He pointed at her. "I know that's true." He rolled his shoulders. "All right, let's head out."

Macy fiddled with the buttons that controlled the radio station.

"How about I do that so you can watch the road?" Rhett's fingers brushed against hers as he reached for the controls. He stopped on a popular country song being played on the local station.

As Macy scanned the road, she could see her scar in her peripheral vision where her hand rested on the steering wheel. Rhett's fingers had just traced against that scar. Did he ever think about the day he saved her from the copperhead?

"I saw this guy in concert last year," Rhett offered. "He sounds this good in person."

The voice on the radio came from Clint Oakfield—one of the biggest touring country-western stars at the moment. His first album had gone platinum and the next two had obtained the same distinction even faster than the first.

"It would be great if we could rope someone like him into donating toward the egg hunt." Rhett's statement was delivered in just a matter-of-fact manner; Macy did a quick double take to be sure he wasn't joking. He wasn't. Who was this guy, dreaming big? He almost reminded her of the boy who had once been her best friend.

"How huge would that be?" Macy whispered.

Rhett's laugh was warm and welcoming. "If anyone could do it, you could."

Macy made a mental note to go to Oakfield's website when she got back to the office and see if there was an option to contact his agent or whoever handled his publicity. People had successfully reached out to celebrities on social media before, as well. What would it hurt to try? If he said no they would be no worse off than they were now, but if he said yes? If Clint Oakfield helped in any way at all…it could be a game changer for Red Dog Ranch and all the foster programs. Even if he donated some signed merchandise that they could raffle off, that would be helpful.

"Speaking of donations." Rhett held the clipboard with the list of businesses Macy had wanted to stop in and talk to. He ran a finger down the first section of the list. "All right, we're six for six on places promising donations. Should we try for seven before heading back?" He caught her eye and the grin he sent her way made her stomach somersault. For the last hour in the car he had been her buddy again, joking, smiling and seemingly excited about the challenge of winning over business owners.

A few of the businesses had promised mon-

etary donations; another two were going to donate candy and small prizes to use in the egg
hunt. Yet another promised to rally volunteers
to help man the event.

Macy glanced at the clock on the dashboard
and her heartbeat ratcheted. Fifteen minutes
until she was supposed to meet the Donnelleys at Scoops and Sons for lunch.

And she had yet to inform Rhett about the
meeting.

Hence the erratic heart.

She snuck a glance at him. Okay, the man's
jawline and eyes alone could cause her heart to
go out of control, but that wasn't today's reason. Besides, Rhett had already made it clear
that he should never be the reason for anything
in her life.

The Donnelleys had two adopted children
and two foster kids. Often they had more. Mr.
Donnelley had grown up in the foster system
and had been a teenager when Red Dog Ranch
launched many of its programs. They were
supporters of the ranch, but more than that,
they were friends.

Last night springing a lunch date with the
Donnelleys on Rhett had sounded like such a
good idea. Now? Not so much. Especially not

after they'd stopped by a few local businesses and worked as a team to secure donations.

She and Rhett—a team again.

Macy's mouth felt dry. She needed to tell him. Had to be honest.

Suddenly, Kodiak stood in the back seat and pressed her muzzle into Rhett's ear. Rhett had insisted on bringing her along. Supposedly she didn't do well if she was apart from him for too long, and she had already been outside alone for a chunk of the morning.

Macy couldn't fault Kodiak there.

However, she had the distinct impression that the dog wanted to place herself in between Macy and Rhett as often as she possibly could.

Macy probably should have held her tongue, but she had never been particularly good at doing so. "Ever afraid she might nip you?"

"This brute?" Rhett chuckled and gently nudged Kodiak so she would lie down across the back seat again. "I'd trust her with my life." He held up a hand. "And let's say—theoretically—she did accidentally nip someone. Chessies aren't like other dogs. They're known for their gentle jaws."

"Gentle jaws…on a dog?"

He nodded. "That's why they're perfect birding dogs. They can carry a duck back to you without getting a scratch on it. In fact, a Chessie can be trained to carry an egg in their mouth without breaking it." He jutted his thumb toward the back seat. "Kodiak can."

Macy flipped on the blinker, turning the car in the direction of Scoops and Sons. "You're serious?"

"Of course." His blue eyes lighted with excitement. "With Cassidy's permission, Kodiak has started to learn how to do a water rescue on Piper. She can take an arm or a part of Piper's clothing in her mouth and tow her back to shore. It's pretty amazing. I mean, we only got to try it twice before Piper got hurt. But Kodiak had trained with a dummy at our old place."

Macy couldn't hide the smile that crept onto her face. Rhett's enthusiasm was palpable.

"Okay, you're right. That is amazing." It was great to see him so animated.

"Of course, all that's on hold now. We can't do it again until Piper's cast is off." He frowned. "But I've been having Kodiak practice with other objects." He unbuckled his seat belt without looking toward the restaurant. "She's stronger than she looks—able to haul a lot while she's swimming."

"About Piper." Macy sucked in a sharp

breath as she parked the car in front of the tiny restaurant. "I haven't had a chance to apologize for what happened." She twisted in the seat to face him. "I'm sorry she got hurt and I take full responsibility for what happened."

"Are you trying to convince me to reinstate the interns? Because—"

She touched his wrist. "It was my fault. Mine alone."

"While I appreciate you saying that," he said, shifting the clipboard onto the dashboard and then scrubbing his hand over his face, setting his hat off balance, "I think the fault rests with me. I shouldn't have tried to keep my business going. I should have known continuing to train dogs would only divide my time and attention. I should have been there overseeing the interns. I shoved off that duty—"

"Onto me." Macy pressed her hand against her chest. "And I failed you."

"I doubt you could ever fail me." His voice was so low, so full of emotion, it stirred feelings in Macy's heart she had convinced herself she was doing a good job locking away.

Apparently not.

While Rhett's words threatened to unbind a piece of her heart, she couldn't let that happen. They weren't true. Rhett hadn't wanted her.

He shouldn't say such things.

Her mind suddenly latched onto something else he had said. "Wait. You said you 'shouldn't have tried to keep your business going.' Does that mean—"

"Yes." He tugged his hat off and shoved a hand into his hair. "I have to give up Straight Arrow Retrievers. I don't see any other way around it."

She twisted in her seat, grabbing his arm. "Look at me. You are *not* giving up your business. You care about it too much. It's your passion, Rhett."

"Well, it's not humanly possible to run the ranch, the foster programs, and manage my family and Straight Arrow Retrievers at the same time. Not well. Not successfully. Something has to give and I don't see what else I can cut." He tipped his head back against the headrest.

Her heart went out to him. If only she could convince him to share his burdens. He didn't have to manage everything alone. He wasn't alone at all.

"You have a staff, Rhett. Delegate the ranch duties. We can make this work."

He turned his head in her direction. "You

know, you make me believe it could almost work. That's dangerous, Mace."

She smiled. "I've never been a fan of safe."

Rhett swallowed hard. While they'd been able to make progress for the egg hunt, spending time alone with Macy was messing with his head. Oh, he wanted to keep talking with her. Wanted to keep making her smile and laugh. Wanted to keep hearing her encouragement.

That was the problem.

Friendship with Macy was far too risky.

Macy was determined and hardworking and positive. She was passionate about important things and was willing to fight for what mattered to her. She was beautiful, but then she always had been. He had simply been too bullheaded to allow himself to notice for fear of what it would do to their friendship.

How many things had he lost because of choices made from fear?

But fear—caution—kept a person safe. In the horror movies it was always the brave person who went out to investigate a noise who got the ax first, not the vigilant ones hiding inside. They were smart. They stayed safe. Alive.

Walls and hiding were good things. No one could tell him differently.

Because the truth was Rhett could very easily lose his heart to Macy for good if he wasn't careful. So he would be careful. He had to be. He had too much to juggle, too much riding on his shoulders without additional complications.

Besides, she had rejected him before.

He had to keep reminding himself of that. It was the one thought that could protect him. He stole a glance at her as she used the rear-view mirror to fix her hair.

Perhaps the only thing.

He looked through the window, finally taking in where they'd parked: Scoops and Sons, a great diner off the beaten path of town. While out-of-towners more than likely assumed the place was simply an ice cream shop, it was so much more. Scoops was a mom-and-pop eatery that served up some of the best brisket sandwiches and corn cobbler Rhett had ever eaten.

"I like this place." Rhett plucked the clipboard from the dashboard. "But it isn't on the list."

Macy sighed. "Okay, don't be mad."

Never a good way to start.

"Why would I be mad?" In response to his

tone, Kodiak sat up in the back seat and let out a low whine.

Macy nervously looked from his dog to him. "I should have said something sooner. We're meeting someone here for lunch. I didn't think it would be a big deal."

Rhett scooted the clipboard back onto the dash. The metal clip caught the sunlight, sending a prism onto the car's ceiling. "That someone being…?"

"Do you remember the Donnelleys?"

Of course he did. Jack Donnelley was a few years older than Rhett and had grown up in the foster system. Jack had been one of the first kids Brock had ever taken under his wing. Rhett's dad had probably spent more time mentoring Jack than he ever had Rhett. Jack had gone on to do well in college, marry a great woman, adopt children from the foster system and continue to foster more. In Brock Jarrett's eyes Jack was as successful as a man could be.

Everything Rhett wasn't.

Rhett narrowed his eyes. He had a hard time believing Macy had forgotten about the animosity between him and Jack. For senior night at Rhett's final football game, Rhett had begged his father to attend. *Just this once, Dad.*

Please. Everyone else's parents had come to all the games, but Brock rarely had. *I would, son, but I have to meet with this family...this other kid needs me.* There had always been a million reasons why he couldn't be there—good reasons, ones that made Rhett feel bad about himself when he looked out into the stands, didn't see his dad and tasted disappointment. His dad was tied up with something more important than football.

More important than him.

Rhett shouldn't have been hurt. He was supposed to be old enough to understand that the needs of others were more important than his silly wants and desires. Whatever Rhett was doing was insignificant in his father's eyes. Always had been.

Probably still was.

Rhett rubbed at his jaw.

The last game? Brock had chosen to help Jack Donnelley pack his apartment and move to Red Dog Ranch instead of attending. His dad had missed the awards ceremony. Missed all the nice things Coach had said about Rhett.

Not that it would have mattered.

Rhett's focus snapped back to Macy.

"If you did this to try to convince me to reinstate the intern program," he said, "I already decided to do that." After talking with Cassidy he had realized she was right. He had sent emails to set up meetings to go over new safety protocols with all the staff members who had been appointed as mentors, and after those meetings took place tomorrow he would send emails to all the student interns inviting them back to the ranch.

Macy's eyebrows went up. "You—you did? Why didn't you say something?"

"I tried to tell you earlier, but you cut me off."

She cringed. "I do that a lot, don't I?"

He suppressed a good-natured laugh because he was certain that wouldn't have been appreciated during the type of conversation they were engaged in. But, honestly, Macy had been cutting him off since she had been old enough to learn to speak. It was a part of her personality—overexcited, passionate, always charging ahead. That was... Macy. It was who she was and he would never want her to be anyone different.

He shrugged. "You always have. Usually it's endearing."

Her eyes went wide. She opened her mouth to say something.

But he couldn't go down that road. He

shouldn't have admitted that he found any-thing about her endearing. Life was far too complicated at the moment to let anyone in.

Especially Macy Howell.

Before she could respond, Rhett hooked his fingers over the handle and pushed it open. "Well, let's get on with it then. We don't want to keep them waiting."

She rounded to his side of the car while he was letting Kodiak out.

"You'll still go in and have lunch?" she asked.

Rhett forced a smile. "As long as the Don-nelleys are good with eating on the patio where Kodiak is allowed."

"You're sure?" she pressed.

"Listen." Kodiak stopped when he did. "Re-cently I asked God to help me get over this… this grudge, for lack of a better word, that I've had against the foster programs." He shrugged. "Maybe this is part of it. A step in the right direction."

"Rhett, that's—it's huge."

He jerked his chin toward the restaurant. "Let's go."

Jack and Sophie Donnelley welcomed Rhett and Macy with hugs. Their children, Ashton,

Ella, Will and Vicki, were instantly enamored with Kodiak.

"Can we pet her?" Ella's gap-toothed grin reminded him of his nieces.

"Sure." Rhett gestured toward Kodiak. "She loves kids."

After quickly eating, the kids took Kodiak out to a large grassy patch that ran alongside the restaurant. The patio overlooked the area so the four adults were able to keep an eye on them. Sophie had unearthed a tennis ball from somewhere in the recesses of their minivan and Kodiak was living the retriever's dream with four kids willing to play fetch with her.

Jack leaned back in his chair. "I have to tell you, we were worried about what would happen to the ranch after your father passed. You know, I always thought of him as my father figure too."

Rhett worked his jaw back and forth. He forced out a breath. "Yeah, I hear that a lot."

"Oh, I'm sure." Jack's smile was genuine. He had always been kind, which only made Rhett feel worse about himself for ever having disliked the man. "I haven't seen you in a while, but it feels like we haven't missed a beat. I guess that's because your dad spoke about you all the time."

Rhett caught Macy's eye. "He—he did?"

Jack nodded. "I know he loved all his kids equally, but you held a special place in his heart."

"He was so proud of your dog business," Sophie chimed in.

Rhett's throat felt raw.

Was it all true? Rhett had a hard time wrapping his mind around the idea. When Brock had given him the ultimatum and Rhett had chosen to leave, Brock had been red-faced, yelling. Brock had been the complete opposite of proud. Even after they had patched their relationship back together for Mom's sake, Rhett and his father had forged a tense truce at best.

Not once had Brock looked him in the eye and said he was proud.

Not once had he showed up for a competition that included one of the dogs Rhett had trained.

Rhett let his gaze drift to the field where the kids were playing with Kodiak. His heart twisted. Seeing their joy, their innocence—no, he couldn't harbor a grudge against the foster programs any longer. The kids were blameless in all that had happened to him.

"Ashton's looking forward to his first year at Camp Firefly." Jack rose from his seat to lean on the patio's railing. "We were worried you might end some of the programs your dad had started. New leadership sometimes has different priorities." Jack almost sounded like he was apologizing for judging Rhett incorrectly.

If only he knew how close he had come to striking the truth.

Rhett sighed. The Donnelleys were good people who deserved honesty. "Programs remain the same for now, but we are looking at possibly cutting back." Rhett rushed on, "These things are expensive. Take the egg hunt for example. We've been all over town this morning soliciting donations—and we did well—but it will probably need to be downsized."

Jack turned to face them. "If you still need one, I could probably get you a helicopter for the candy drop, free of charge."

Macy had been reaching for her sweet tea and now her hand froze. "Are you for real?"

Sophie looked as if she might burst with pride. She leaned toward Rhett and Macy. "Jack just got promoted to sergeant in the Aircraft Operations Division. He's one of their pilots now."

Rhett had forgotten Jack was an officer with the Texas Department of Public Safety. He certainly hadn't known the man could fly a helicopter though. "If you're sure, I won't turn down an offer like that."

"It shouldn't be a problem," Jack assured them. "My department encourages us to participate in charity events."

There were hugs when everyone finally decided to part ways. Rhett invited the Donnelleys to stop by the ranch whenever they wanted to, and Sophie promised they would take him up on the offer.

Sophie laughed. "Now that the kids have met Kodiak you know they're going to be begging to see her again."

Chapter Six

Rhett left the office early the next day to check on the interns. Yesterday, after he and Macy had returned home, they had made quick work of the phone calls on his to-do list and had been able to meet with all the staff mentors before dinner, making it possible for the interns to come back today.

Gabe and a few of the others had been assigned to help on the maintenance crew, so Rhett drove one of the four-wheelers out to the fence line where the crew was trimming the long grasses and weeds. Staff had to keep them short so gates between pastures would be easier to use.

Normally he would have walked out to the spot, but at the last minute Rhett had decided to strap a cooler filled with ice-cold water bottles to the back of the four-wheeler. It was only March, but the afternoons got hot.

Rhett found Gabe and the others were working hard under the direction of an aged ranch hand. After confirming with the older man, Rhett had to admit Gabe was a good kid.

Gabe used the back of his wrist to swipe sweat from his brow. "Boss, if you don't mind me asking, how's Piper doing?"

Rhett handed the youth a fresh water bottle. "Nothing fazes that little girl." He pointed at the teenager. "Speaking of, make sure you swing by the mess hall and sign her cast before you leave today."

Gabe saluted him.

"And, Gabe?" Rhett cleared his throat. "I know you have your heart set on becoming a veterinarian." The teenager nodded. "Come see me after you're done here and we can talk about putting you on rotation with everyone who works with the animals so you get a chance to see all sides. I'd be happy to show you what I do for dog training, as well, if that's something you'd be interested in."

Satisfied that the teenager was in good hands, Rhett headed back toward the house. Kodiak happily bounded beside his vehicle the whole way. He left the four-wheeler in its usual place near the pole barn and was about to make his way to the ranch house to see how his mom was doing when he spotted Shannon crouched where they stored the hay bales.

As he entered the barn his boots crunched on gravel, alerting Shannon to his presence. Her head snapped up and her blotchy red cheeks gave her away. Rhett's stomach clenched. She'd been crying, sobbing by the looks of it. Seeing her that way made his heart feel wrung out.

What had he missed?

"Hey." He hastened his steps. "What's wrong?" He sat beside her, his arm instinctively going around her shoulders. Every protective impulse flared inside of him. Were the tears because of her boyfriend, Cord Anders? And if so…was it horrible that Rhett would be happy if they had broken up? Rhett had noticed Shannon changing, shrinking into herself ever since she had started dating the man. If he had his way, he would ban the guy from the ranch. He shoved the thought away. Right now all that mattered was Shannon was upset. He needed to be empathetic no matter the reason for her tears. His sister deserved nothing less.

She dropped her head into her hands and her shoulders shook a few times. "Nothing. I don't know." Her voice pitched higher. "Everything."

Not knowing what to say, he rubbed his hand in a circle against her back.

"I'm so stupid," Shannon breathed out.

"Shh." Rhett pulled her to his side in a hug. "No one talks about my favorite sister like that. Not even my favorite sister."

A watery laugh escaped her lips. "I'm your only sister."

"What's wrong?" he whispered the question again.

She shoved her blond curls away from her face. "I'm losing everything." She looked away, out the barn doors. Her eyes focused on something far in the distance or maybe nothing at all; Rhett couldn't tell.

His gut clenched. He had never seen his sister despairing.

Help me, Lord.

"First there was Wade—" her voice strained over her twin's name "—then Dad." She wiped at another tear. "Now it's Mom."

Rhett's fingers tightened over her shoulder. The Jarretts had experienced their share of losses over the last few years, but they would weather them together. Shannon had to know that. He would always be there for her, no matter what happened.

"Mom's still here," he said. "We still have time with her."

Shannon's head swung back around, her gaze latching onto his as if he could save her from drowning. "Not really, Rhett. You and I both know that. She's not usually *there*. Not anymore. I can't go talk to her. I can't—" Her face crumpled. "I feel like I'm losing myself. I'm so—" A sob broke from her chest. Loud and full of long pent-up pain.

Kodiak pranced nearby, her low, sharp whimpers joining Shannon's tears.

Rhett gathered his sister to his chest. If only there was something he could say to make everything better for her. But he knew words didn't have that type of power. In his life words had always caused far more pain than healing. Only actually being there for a person helped, and if he was being honest, he had failed Shannon in the past on that count. He hadn't been around to support her during the most difficult days at Red Dog Ranch.

He refused to fail her now.

She clung to his arms and shoved her forehead into his collarbone. "Nothing makes me happy. Nothing makes me smile anymore. Everything keeps changing and I hate it, and I hate that I can't handle it."

His sister's words gutted him completely. Rhett wrapped his arms more securely around her. "I'm here," he whispered over and over.

She slammed her palms against him and scooted away. "For how long this time?" Her eyes blazed. "You'd sell it in a heartbeat and leave us again if you could. Walk away and never once look back. Never check on us. Never call. Just like before. The only thing keeping you here is Dad's will. We all know that."

"That's not true." His words came out quietly. He would never walk away from his family again, but he couldn't blame her for making a logical jump based on his past actions. He had left her to bear the burden of their mom's illness and deal with their parents alone after Boone and his family left for seminary. She had been the one the police made a death notice to—alone. How secluded she must have felt, entirely deserted by all her brothers. Rhett could never repay her and now it was evident how much it had taxed her, how much he would forever be indebted to his sister. The knowledge hollowed out his chest.

"You don't care about me. Not really."

"I love you. You know that. I'm sorry for—"

She shot to her feet. "You're trying to get out of the will. I know you are."

"Shannon." Rhett slowly rose to his feet. He put his hands out, the same way he would have approached a scared animal. "When I left? That was an issue between me and Dad. I had a beef with him—no one else." He took a step closer. "You have no idea how sorry I am about the past. I ask your forgiveness for not being here, not supporting you better in all the ways I should have."

"Cord's right." Shannon crossed her arms. "None of you care. Not really."

Cord. Of course.

Rhett's movement stilled.

"Is that where this is all coming from?" he asked, hoping for the truth. Praying he could get through to her about her boyfriend. "That guy is bad news. You've been hurting ever since you got with him. That's not love, Shannon. Love heals people—it doesn't destroy them. I don't think he's right for you."

"He's the only good thing in my life right now." Her voice rose. "And now you're trying to take that away from me too. He warned me this would happen."

"That's absurd." Maybe not his best, most caring word choice. Rhett started again, more kindly. "There are so many people here who love you. If this guy has made you think differently then—"

She let out a derisive laugh. "Cord was right. The whole family is against me. I should have known better than to even bother to try to get you to understand." Shannon turned.

Rhett followed after her. "We're not done."

She sliced him with a glare. "Do you think you're Dad now? Because that's hilarious, Rhett." Her voice was ice. This was not any version of the Shannon he knew. It made a creeping sensation go up his back. "You don't have the right to step into our lives and think you can solve all our problems or be some makeshift patriarch now. If you think that's what we want, well, you're wrong. You could never fill Dad's shoes. Not even close. So don't even try."

"I know that," he said quietly. "I'm not trying to be Dad, but I do want to do the best I can by you. By me. By God. I can't undo the past but I can promise that I will never walk away from you again."

She left and this time he didn't follow her.

While he stared after Shannon's retreating form, Kodiak shoved her nose into Rhett's hand. Shannon was right—Rhett had failed them in the past. All of them, but especially Shannon. He pushed his fingers into Kodiak's coarse fur. Resolve forming.

He had a chance to right the wrongs both he and his father had committed.

For far too long the Jarretts had placed Brock on a pedestal because he was a good man with a big heart. But in a way, their dad had failed them most of all. He had put so many things—admirable things—ahead of his family. From Wade's attention-seeking youth, which had led him down a bad path, arguably resulting in his death, to Rhett's constant struggle with rejection and to Shannon's obvious emotional pain, which had driven her to a man like Cord, it didn't take a genius to see how much Brock's lack of attention had cost their family. Happily married, Boone seemed to be the only one to have escaped a measure of dysfunction, but then again, maybe Boone just hid it better.

Rhett would stay and make the ranch a success. If the lawyer could find a loophole in the will, he would be able to show his family that they—not any program or charity—came first. Rhett would figure out the balance between caring for them and helping people in need, because he was starting to think it was possible to do both. It had to be.

He would prove Shannon wrong on another point too. He would be there when Cord Anders broke her heart. He was willing to weather years of her barbs and pained words if that was what he had to do to prove to her that he was no longer the man who walked away.

Even though the path was well illuminated by a flood lamp hanging near the barns, Macy could have walked the path from her bungalow to the big house with her eyes closed. The door to the Jarretts' house had been open to her since she was a baby and it had become her favorite place when they warmly welcomed her after her mother's sudden death. Macy had only been eighteen and would have been left utterly alone in the world if the Jarretts hadn't ushered her into their fold.

If they hadn't made her a part of their family.

At one time, she had believed she might really become a Jarrett. Until the bottom fell out and she tasted bitter reality about her friendship with Rhett. Friends, only ever friends.

For so many years, their home had been her home…except she hadn't set foot inside since

Rhett had been back. It was his domain now and she had not wanted to encroach.

Cassidy had texted Macy twice during the day, reminding her about the planned movie night in the big house. Why had she agreed to go in the first place? Sure, it would be nice to spend time with Shannon, Cassidy and, if she was feeling up to it, Mrs. Jarrett, but there were things she could be handling in the office. More work to get done.

A dog's bark made her jump. With a small yelp, Macy whirled around. When she squinted, she could make out Rhett and Kodiak walking up from the lake. And was that… she squinted more… Romeo the miniature donkey with them?

Rhett's posture changed the second he caught sight of her, but he relaxed his shoulders a moment later. "Out for a stroll in your pajamas?" he hollered since they were still a ways away, his voice warm.

Macy glanced down, mortified. Her pajama pants were covered with brightly colored T. rexes trying to hug each other but not being able to because of their short arms, and she wore a shirt with big letters that read Surely Not Everybody Was Kung Fu Fighting. Summoning her dignity, Macy trudged through the bluebonnets toward him. At least she wasn't wearing her cow slippers.

"Nice shirt." Rhett handed her Romeo's lead rope. "Where are you headed?"

Macy jerked her thumb to point over her shoulder toward the Jarretts' house. "Girls night. We're watching Cary Grant."

"Ah, yes. Now that you mention it, I seem to recall Cassidy telling me I wasn't allowed in my own living room tonight." His eyes narrowed. "Are those dinosaurs on your pants or are they llamas?"

"No more clothing comments unless you want me to turn this around and make fun of you." She fell into step beside Rhett as they headed in the direction of the nearby barn where Romeo and the miniature horse, Sheep, spent their nights.

Rhett made a show of pretending offense. He glanced down as if taking in his own boots, jeans and button-down. "All right, do your worst. What do you have to say about this?"

Macy stopped and looked at Rhett. The man was all cowboy—broad shouldered, tough muscled, with a shadow of end-of-the-day stubble dusting his chin. She fought the sudden itch to touch his jaw. To run her finger along the planes of his face, back into the hair that curled out from under his hat. His bright blue eyes drew her in and Macy's gaze went to his lips. She sucked in a sharp breath and took a step back.

Even in friendship they had never been forward with each other. Plenty of high fives and backslaps sprinkled with the occasional hugs, but other than the one time he had carried her after the snakebite, there had never been a touch that held meaning beyond "Well done" or "Good to see you."

Well, besides that one kiss.

"I, ah, I can't." Suddenly nervous, she swallowed hard. "You always look, um, really… attractive." Heat flared on her neck and her cheeks.

Attractive. She'd really just said that.

Out loud.

Rhett's laugh was warm. "Attractive, huh? Why do I get the sense you're buttering me up to ask a favor or something? Go on," he joked. "What do you want?"

You. Just you. Even though you're the most stubborn, exasperating man I've ever met. It's always been you. It will only ever be you.

Romeo butted his head into her back, shoving her closer to Rhett. Rhett dropped a hand onto her shoulder, ensuring the small donkey wouldn't be able to push Macy again. However, Rhett kept his hold even after Romeo started munching at a patch of clover.

Macy tipped her head to meet Rhett's eyes. She licked her lips. "Come on, you have to know by now how handsome you are."

Instead of answering, Rhett cocked his head and studied her.

He was so close and for the first time since returning to the ranch, something about him was different. It felt as if his heart wasn't entirely locked up tonight. She imagined it as a door only slightly ajar, but maybe she could wedge a foot in. Maybe she could make some progress with him. Maybe she could win her friend back.

Kodiak shoved her way in between them. She sat directly on the tips of Rhett's boots and stared up at Macy, her muzzle inches away from Macy's thigh.

Macy groaned. "I get the feeling your dog doesn't like me much."

Rhett's gaze drifted over Macy's features, lingering on her mouth. A shy smile lighted his face, causing the skin around his eyes to crinkle. "She's, ah, jealous."

"Of me?" Macy gripped Romeo's lead line

a little harder than necessary. "I can't imagine why."

Rhett's smile widened. "Really?"

A part of Macy wanted to press Rhett to clarify, but a bigger part of her brain screamed a warning. It couldn't be what she hoped. Rhett could never care about her in the same way she cared about him. If he had, their kiss would have gone far differently.

Why did you do that? Why did you do that?

Macy needed to steer the conversation to safer waters for both of their sakes. Rhett was her boss, he had emphatically told her he didn't want to be friends again, and she still wasn't sure if he was on board with saving all the foster programs long-term.

Further talk in this direction would only end with her hurt again.

Macy's thumb instinctively found the scar on her finger.

Rhett sighed, clearly disappointed that she hadn't continued their conversation. But she couldn't go down that road with him. She refused to press him about why Kodiak would be jealous of her. Any chance Rhett and her could have had at a relationship ended three years ago. Besides, Rhett had just started to warm up to her again—to smile and joke with her like the old days. She wouldn't let anything harm the chance to mend their friendship. Not even her desire for answers and closure about *what might have been*.

She had to change the topic and head up to the house. Macy pivoted to face the barn. "Sheep's probably missing Romeo."

Rhett's Adam's apple bobbed. "Right." He scrubbed a hand over his face. "Let's put him to bed then."

With Kodiak on his heels, Rhett fell into step next to Macy. His ever-present shadow made Macy remember something else she had been meaning to discuss with him.

"I looked up Straight Arrow Retrievers," Macy said with all the casualness she could muster. "Why didn't you tell us about all the awards you won? You trained Benny—that dog went to big award shows as a presenter."

Rhett unlatched the barn door and held it open as she led Romeo inside. He took his time catching up. "Would any of it have mattered?" His voice was quiet, almost a whisper.

By the time he came up behind her, Macy had ushered Romeo into his stall. She spun around, finding Rhett closer than she had thought he would be. "Of course it matters.

Your accomplishments are worth celebrating. You can't give it up."

"I don't see how I can keep training dogs with everything else I have going on."

"I've watched you out there in the field with them." She poked his chest. "You're happy. Really happy when you're working dogs. I don't want you to lose that."

He pinched the bridge of his nose. "I don't want to talk about this right now. Other things—" his gaze dipped to her mouth "—but not this."

"Then what do you want to talk about?" The second the question passed her lips she wished she hadn't voiced it. She should have said good-night and gone on her way, but his eyes were pleading with her and looking away was near impossible.

He eased the lead line from Macy's grasp, his eyes never leaving hers. "Why didn't you return my calls?"

Unwelcome nerves jangled through her. "You honestly want to have this conversation?" What if they ruined all the headway they had made? Of all the things for him to want to discuss. "Because last time I brought it up you seemed pretty opposed to it."

He stepped back and looped the lead line

back on a peg with some other equipment. "I left you so many messages." His back was to her. His shoulders rose on a shaky breath. "For so long you just ignored them—ignored me. I still can't wrap my head around what happened."

"I was embarrassed, Rhett." She threw out her arms. "What did you expect me to do after that?"

Rhett finally turned around. "I wanted you to talk with me." His voice was even. "Friends do that. They talk through things. Do you know how much I missed you the last few years?"

Friends.

And there it was: Confirmation. Friends. Just friends. All he would ever consider her. Why she should have walked away ten minutes ago. Why she had to end this conversation before she was forced to admit to her feelings.

"I wasn't going to take the job," she said, but it sounded lame even to her own ears.

A wrinkle formed between his eyes. "This has nothing to do with the job offer." He took a half step in her direction. "Are you honestly going to keep pretending you don't know what I'm getting at?"

Macy crossed her arms over her chest. "You

didn't call me back either. You know, the path goes both ways."

He took off his hat and ran a shaky hand through his hair. "You called once, Macy. Once. *Five* months later."

Kodiak raised her head and whimpered.

Rhett looked at Kodiak, back at Macy, away again. "I shouldn't have raised my voice. I'm sorry, I'm just dealing with a lot here."

"Like what?"

"Shannon hates me." His voice trembled. "She hates me, Mace." He shook his head when she opened her mouth. "And you? Whenever I think…" He backed away. "I'm sorry. I shouldn't have said anything. There's so much on my mind tonight. Forget all this for me."

He was gone before she could say anything else. Between what seemed like flirtation at the beginning of their interaction to the bombshell about Shannon and his obvious hurt, it was hard to wade through what she should think and feel about it all. She was relieved he hadn't pressed talking about their kiss more. Their friendship was just starting to feel comfortable again and a long talk about why he would never think of her romantically would only make her pull away. As much as she wished it was otherwise, they needed to go on as if the kiss had never happened.

She could be his friend again.

Just friends.

It would be enough.

It would have to be enough.

Macy stood in the barn's doorway long after she lost sight of him.

Chapter Seven

When Macy stretched, her spine answered with a series of little popping noises. Sleeping on the floor as a twenty-eight-year-old was a significantly different experience than all the times she had done so at sleepovers as a teenager. Her joints wouldn't thank her.

After her conversation with Rhett, Macy had gone ahead with her planned movie night with the other girls. If only because she'd known Cassidy was bound to show up at her house and drag her, kicking and screaming, to the Jarrett house if Macy had dared to text to cancel. Even still she had been tempted.

Thankfully, Rhett was safely tucked away upstairs when she arrived and stayed that way the rest of the evening while Cassidy, Shannon, Piper and Macy watched movies and consumed a shocking amount of popcorn and chocolate. As usual, Piper was asleep within the first ten minutes of the first movie. Somewhere between watching *To Catch a Thief* and Macy's favorite Cary Grant movie, *Charade*, they all decided to turn the marathon into a sleepover and added *Houseboat* to the lineup.

A wall of windows on one side of the room showed a pink-and-gold wash of sunrise cresting over the hills. Cassidy and Piper were still snoozing together on the large couch, but Shannon's spot in the recliner was empty. Had she gone upstairs to her own room at some point or had she snuck out to meet with Cord? Shannon had been present last night but not engaged.

Rhett and his sister had to have had words yesterday because it wasn't like Rhett to throw around the word *hate*. A sick feeling swam through Macy. She had considered pulling Shannon aside many times throughout the last few weeks, but the time had never felt right. She needed to be a better friend to Shannon in the future.

Keep Shannon safe, Lord. Help her see how much You love her. Help us get through to her. And whatever's going on between her and Rhett—please heal their hurt. She was about to end her plea but then added, *Could You help me with Rhett too? I'm not sure what's going on. I'm not even sure what's happening in my own life anymore.*

Macy had plugged her phone in to charge on the kitchen counter before she had fallen asleep. With all the emails she had sent out recently regarding the foster programs, she liked to check for responses first thing each morning. After getting home from Scoops and Sons, she had sent a message to Clint Oakfield. Was it silly to hope he would respond?

She rose only to spot Mrs. Jarrett peacefully sitting at the head of the dining-room table. The woman looked over at her and smiled serenely. Macy was once again struck by how cruel Alzheimer's was. From the outside, Rhett's mom appeared the same as ever.

It was a shock to see her up and about before her nurse arrived. How long had she been there? Mrs. Jarrett hadn't been well enough to join them last night. But here she was, hands folded over her open Bible, bright and early in the morning, smiling at Macy as if she had been waiting for her. The woman had a way of looking regal, even in her brown robe with her white hair slightly mussed with sleep. Macy crossed into the kitchen, socks padding over the hardwood floor. "Can I get something for you?"

Mrs. Jarrett touched the spot to her right. "Just come and sit with me, dear."

Macy filled two cups with water and brought them to the table. "How are you doing this morning?"

A glass jar on the table held a fragrant bouquet of Texas sage, orange jubilee and gold lantana. Cassidy had told Macy that Rhett picked a new bouquet of flowers at the ranch for his mother every couple of days.

Mrs. Jarrett fanned her fingers over the thin pages of her open Bible. "If you're asking if today is a good day or a bad day for my mind—today I remember. I know myself."

Swallowing hard, Macy glanced toward the staircase and wondered if she should rouse Rhett or Shannon. She knew they would appreciate some time with their mother during a lucid moment. Macy bit her lip. Another part of her wondered if she should broach the topic of Rhett's adoption with Mrs. Jarrett. Every time Macy sat at her desk and looked at the photo of Brock at the opening of Camp Firefly she fought the urge to go into Rhett's office and confess what she knew. Rhett deserved to know the truth about his parentage, but she couldn't break her promise to Brock.

No matter how often she wanted to.

Rhett's mom gazed toward the stairs. "They're both already gone for the day. Rhett left very early. More so than usual. It makes a person wonder why." Mrs. Jarrett trained her focus on Macy. "When will you two give in and get married already?"

Macy choked on the sip of water she had just taken. She covered her mouth.

Unfazed, Rhett's mom continued, "My thickheaded boy may not realize it, but he's loved you his whole life. Still does. I think more now than ever. Some people love each other for a season or while it's convenient, but you two share the growing kind of love—it keeps getting bigger and deeper."

Macy considered acting as if she had no clue what Mrs. Jarrett was talking about, but why? The Jarrett matriarch was lucid, but lately these were rare moments. Macy had always cherished the woman's wisdom and perspective. She wouldn't forsake an opportunity to speak with the lady who had become her second mom.

She filled her lungs with air, let it out. "I'm pretty sure my feelings are no secret, but Rhett never went down that road. I always figured if it was meant to be, it would happen." She shrugged, trying to pretend the admission didn't sting. "So I guess it wasn't meant to be."

"'If it's meant to be'?" Mrs. Jarrett snorted and batted her hand in the air. "What hogwash. Love is work. Hard work. It's late-night tears and fights and forgiving and choosing a person even on their worst days. I've never known such pain as the pain of love. 'Meant to be,'" she grumbled again, as if the words offended her. "Anyone who treats it so carelessly has never truly known it."

Macy's eyes burned. Tears had gathered as Mrs. Jarrett spoke. "When Rhett left the ranch—" Her voice cracked. "He knew me better than anyone and rejected me."

Rhett's mom nodded thoughtfully. "And he will likely hurt you again and you him. That's how living goes." She tapped the table. "That's especially how loving goes."

Macy straightened her spine. "Which is exactly why it would never work for us."

"Sweet child, don't you know?" Mrs. Jarrett covered Macy's hand with both of hers. "God's love is the only one that never lets us down. All others will at some point. We're human, you realize." She cupped her hands around Macy's. "I made mistakes with Brock and the good Lord knows Brock let us down sometimes too. Rhett will do the same and maybe you don't want to hear it, but you will stumble in relationships too—for the rest of your life, my dear. I'm sorry to be the one to tell you these things."

"I know I'm not perfect—"

"*None* of us are." She winked. "But I find that's part of the adventure."

"Do you know he's trying to downsize the foster programs? He would have cut the egg hunt if I hadn't convinced him not to." Macy felt like she was tattling on Rhett. She knew he wouldn't have discussed these things with his mom, but Mrs. Jarrett had been a driving force for establishing Camp Firefly, among other things, and deserved a voice in the matter.

His mom released Macy's hand so she could trace her finger over a highlighted line in her Bible. "I wonder, does your push to save the things Brock started come from a place of love or do you believe it's your burden, your badge of honor—your pride at stake?" She caressed the highlighted page again. "Right here, 'do all things out of love.' It sounds so easy, but it is the hardest thing that will ever be asked of us because love...love is sometimes the most painful feeling on earth, child. But it's worth it. We have the proof right here." She closed her Bible and tapped the cover. "It's worth every sacrifice, every arrow sent into the soft part of our heart. It's worth it."

As the nurse arrived Macy kissed Mrs. Jarrett on the cheek. "Thank you for your wisdom."

Mrs. Jarrett caught her hand, giving it an extra squeeze before letting go. As Macy left, she blinked away tears. She forced down the emotions talking with Mrs. Jarrett had stirred. But even after Macy had showered, changed and headed into the office, she couldn't shake the oldest Jarrett's words.

Macy and Rhett had hurt each other, but did that mean their entwined story had to end? Macy didn't want it to.

She wished she would have handled last night differently. Been honest. Vulnerable.

If she had been brave and spoken her heart then at least she would know now. She wouldn't be stuck in the Land of Maybe any longer. The truth could have been used to guide her.

Macy finally focused on her phone; an email sparked her interest. She let out a long stream of air. She couldn't wait to tell Rhett about this.

* * *

Rhett brushed his hand over his eyes, hoping no one would be able to notice the lingering hint of tears later on. He hadn't meant to wake up early and visit his father's grave, but here he was.

Rhett knelt in front of the headstone and traced his fingers over his father's name and the small dash in between the date of birth and date of death. The small dash that symbolized his life. It was in the dash that Brock had raised and loved Rhett despite both men's failings. Brock might have dropped the ball in many aspects of fatherhood, but Rhett had never doubted his father's love.

Humid air draped around Rhett's shoulders, causing his shirt to stick to his back. A light breeze rustled flowers placed on nearby grave sites and a colorful pinwheel twirled in the wind, stuck into the ground near a tombstone with birth and death dates painfully close together. If it wasn't for the occasional gusts it would have felt like a summer morning outside instead of the end of March.

"Why me?" Rhett whispered. "Why did you leave the ranch to me? It makes no sense. You had no reason to trust me, to believe in me after—" His voice broke. "After I walked away. I'm so sorry I didn't make it to the hospital in time to say goodbye." He had immediately gotten into his truck and headed for home when Shannon had called him about the accident. But a hundred miles was too far. Too long. His father had passed on fifteen minutes before he parked at the hospital. "I'm sorry, Dad. I'm so sorry I didn't get to say goodbye. Hug you one more time." Tears fell now. *Let them.*

His phone buzzed in his pocket and he tugged it out. It was a text from Jack Donnelley—an image of all of Jack's kids with their arms wrapped around Kodiak as they smiled at the camera. His text said the dog was a perfect mascot for Red Dog Ranch.

Macy had once said the same exact thing.

Rhett turned his phone to silent and tucked it back away.

After a few more minutes Rhett found his way to his truck and eased into the front seat. Why had it taken him so long to visit the grave site?

Last night after talking to Macy, Rhett had gone back to his room, but sleep hadn't come. He had stared up at the ceiling watching the fan blades whip around and thought about all that had gone wrong in his life. If he hadn't frozen that night three years ago with Macy they could have been together now. He might have been home years earlier.

But he couldn't force Macy to talk about their past any more than he could fix Shannon's problems. All night one thought kept pounding through his head—with so much of his life spinning out of control, he needed to focus on the few things he had power over. The biggest being his own heart. Hadn't he asked God to help heal his grudge against the ranch? A piece of that was making peace with his father. Visiting his grave had been the only way Rhett could think to do that.

Without turning his truck on, he gripped the steering wheel and shoved his forehead against it. A sudden throb radiated through his chest, making him gasp for breath. Would life always feel like such a mess? Shannon and the ranch and Mom and Macy. Rhett thought of the Donnelleys—how the ranch had helped Jack when he was younger and how much his kids were looking forward to camp. Rhett's heart twisted. Those kids deserved a place like Camp Firefly. Kids like Gabe deserved a safe space too.

He had asked God to help him release his

grudge—coming to terms with his mixed emotions for his father was a piece of moving forward.

Here in the graveyard where thoughts tended to drift toward legacies and how important it was to live with meaning, Rhett finally saw his excuses for what they were—thinly veiled childhood bitterness that he had held on to for so many years. A little boy who wanted his dad to look his way and offer a proud smile, who had wanted to know he came first, if only once. It would never happen, not with Brock gone, and Rhett had to accept that or remain stuck forever.

What was the point of hoarding bad memories, allowing them to take up space in his heart and mind—crowding his life so much that there wasn't room for other things?

Happy, hopeful things.

Rhett was tired of the heavy chains that came with resentment. He didn't want them in his life anymore. Someday, when his body would wind up in a plot not far from his father's, he wanted to know his time had counted. If there was a balance between providing for his family and continuing the events of the ranch, Rhett would find it. He would help heal his family too, if he could.

However, he knew it would be impossible to accomplish any of those things outside of God. Rhett had neglected his relationship with God for far too long. He would never get the last talk or hug with his earthly dad, but he could mend things with God the Father. It was time to go back to church again, time to dust off his Bible and time to open a line of communication through prayer. No matter how strange or strained it might feel, he knew God was there, waiting. Always had been.

Maybe Brock had been too. Rhett would never know because he had squandered the chance to truly reconcile. A mistake he wouldn't make again. Not with God or Shannon or Macy. Not with anyone, if it was up to him. Life was too short, too unpredictable, to hold grudges or allow miscommunications to ruin relationships.

Rhett headed back to the ranch. He had only just parked his vehicle when he caught sight of Macy cutting through the field of bluebonnets toward him. Kodiak trotted at Macy's side, a red ball in her mouth. The two of them looked as if they were racing to put out a fire. The dog was probably miffed at being left behind, but it wouldn't have been respectful to have her in the cemetery and it would have been far too hot to leave her in the vehicle. Rhett exited his truck and strolled to the fence line to meet them.

Macy huffed. "Where have you been? When I saw Kodiak was here but not your truck, I freaked out." Her brows lowered. "And you need to start answering your phone."

Rhett tugged his phone from his pocket. Seven missed calls from Macy. He had turned the vibrate function off after Jack's text had interrupted him. "It was on silent." Her scowl grew and Rhett saw the emotion for what it was—concern. He quickly added, "Sorry if I worried you."

Macy grabbed his wrist. "I *was* worried." She searched his eyes. "Are you okay? It looks like…" She left it there. "Rhett," she whispered. "I know what you said before, but can't we be friends again?"

He covered her hand with his. He instantly found the scar on her pointer finger and couldn't help but trace over it.

Friends.

The word was too small to capture his feelings for Macy.

She knew every rough part of his personality and yet here she was, asking to be friends. Wanting to be a part of his life even though he had hurt her and let her down more times than he could count. She stood toe-to-toe with him even when they disagreed and challenged him constantly, but only because she believed the best of him.

She believed in him. He let that sink in.

Rhett had loved this woman his entire life.

The realization roared through him, shaking him like a powerful storm.

There had never been another woman on the planet in Rhett's eyes. Only Macy. Always Macy. In the past, he had hidden behind their friendship because he had been fearful of losing her if he made a move. Then last night he had come so close to confessing his feelings, but he was glad he hadn't because Rhett was in no position to start a relationship.

Between his father's death, his mother's health and Shannon's anger, Rhett had so much emotional baggage to deal with before he would be ready to be there for a woman.

To be there for Macy.

If she would even want him.

Rhett scuffed his boot into the dirt.

But he could be her friend, couldn't he? They were already acting like friends anyway. "I'd like to be friends again. I'd like that a lot."

The smile that bloomed on Macy's face was

the most beautiful thing Rhett had ever seen. "Then tell me what's wrong."

There was no point hiding the truth; he was sure she had already read the evidence on his face. "I visited my dad. His grave site."

"I'm proud of you," she said. "I know how hard that can be." She released his wrist and he wished she hadn't. "About last night…"

Rhett scratched at the spot on his neck where his hat met his hairline. "Can we forget last night? I was a bear." He had snapped at her because he was upset over Shannon and he was frustrated Macy wouldn't discuss what had gone wrong three years ago. Since realizing he would have had to put a relationship on hold anyway while he worked through all the emotional issues he was dealing with, now he was thankful the conversation hadn't gone any further.

She poked him in the ribs. "Bears *can* be cuddly."

"Not all bears." He rubbed the spot she had poked as if she had hurt him.

She blew bangs away from her eyes. "Anyway, your roar has never scared me." Macy plucked the ball from Kodiak's mouth and sent it flying. Kodiak went tearing through the field after it. "I don't think she minds me nearly as much when you're not around."

Rhett braced his arms on the top fence railing. "Stick around and she'll consider you family like we all do." Kodiak sometimes took a while to warm up to certain adults, but once she accepted them they became fully her people.

"Speaking of, Sophie Donnelley texted." Macy came up beside him, her shoulder brushing his arm. "She asked if the kids could stop by and see Kodiak today."

"Of course. I said they were always welcome."

His dog had already returned with the ball and dropped it at Macy's feet. When Macy looked Rhett's way with her eyebrows raised in question he jerked his chin toward the ball. Macy winked and scooped it back up again, lobbing it in the other direction.

Macy squinted and held her hand to her brow to block some of the sunshine. "Kodiak was good with those kids."

"She always is."

"Now, I don't know much about training dogs…" Macy's words were measured. She had obviously been thinking about this and wanting to bring it up for some time. "So I don't know if this is an odd suggestion, but did you ever think of training therapy dogs instead of hunting dogs?" She pitched Kodiak's ball again and pressed a hand to his bicep when he opened his mouth to say something. "Hear me out. How Kodiak was with those kids? I feel like she could be a comfort dog for kids in trauma. She could be the comfort dog for the ranch." Macy spread out her arms, encompassing the whole property.

"Red dog." Rhett smiled, remembering what she had said in the chapel last week and what Jack had texted earlier that day.

Macy wagged her finger at him. "I told you she'd make a good mascot."

Rhett wrapped his hand over hers and tugged her a few inches closer. "I should have believed you."

"You usually come around to my ideas." Macy tapped on his chest. "It just takes some pestering."

"That's because they're good ideas." He stepped back, releasing her. If he had stood there a second longer he might have pulled her closer or said something he shouldn't yet. "Honestly? I'd love to train therapy dogs." Probably more than he enjoyed training hunting dogs. "But I just don't know when I'd have the time, and it takes a different sort of train-ing than I know."

Macy leaned her back against the fence so she was facing him. "What if we got you help?"

Rhett scanned the pasture. "We're trying to save money here."

"Hypothetically, if someone took on more of the ranch's responsibilities?"

"Sure, yes." Rhett laughed at her tenacity. "I'd love that. It's a good dream."

She pushed off the fence. "In the meantime, you should reach out to your clients again and schedule more sessions. I can handle some of your load and I'm thinking we should approach Shannon, give her more responsibility."

Rhett considered the idea. Shannon didn't presently have a position at the ranch. "She seems to be going through some stuff right now."

Macy nodded. "I think having duties, things to occupy her other than Cord, would be a good thing."

"It's a good thought. Let me mull it over some." He motioned toward the office. "As for now, I have some calls I have to make. Are you heading over?"

"I actually have to run into town." She

pointed her thumb in the direction of her car. "But I do want to talk with you about something else. Later, of course. I know you're busy."

Rhett felt his eyebrows rise. He fought the urge to press her to talk now, but if she had wanted to talk over something presently she had had an open opportunity and had chosen not to. He could respect her desire to put off whatever she wanted to say until another time. "How about this evening? I take Kodiak to the lake after supper. Would that work?"

She nodded. "That would be perfect."

"Then later it is." He tipped his hat and Kodiak fell into step beside him. He started thinking about ways he could make their meeting tonight special, a sort of olive branch for the new start to their friendship.

"Hey, Rhett," Macy called after him. He turned to find her a few feet away, her fingers entwined. "If you made a promise to someone, a promise you weren't sure you wanted to keep any longer, what would you do?"

A breeze swept down from the hills, making the bluebonnets bob around them. The field resembled a sea of turbulent waves.

He hooked his fingers on his belt. "Talk with the person who I made the promise to, I guess."

"What if that wasn't an option any longer?" She was clearly talking about his dad. Perhaps his visit to Brock's grave had prompted her questions. Rhett couldn't deny his curiosity was piqued, but after his time at the grave site this morning, Rhett knew he needed to work on trusting. Trust that his dad had had good intentions for handing the ranch to him, trust that God had a hand in all the chaos surrounding Rhett's life. Trust Macy too.

Rhett took a half step in her direction. "The person you made the promise to, were they an upright person?"

Macy had been looking down at her hands but now her focus snapped to him. "One of the best I've ever met."

"Then I'd leave it," Rhett said gently.

"You're sure?" She eyed him. "Absolutely sure?"

Rhett knew she was asking something bigger, something more…but he couldn't figure it out. However, if Brock had told her some secret, Rhett wouldn't press her for it. She would only feel guilt after telling him and he couldn't do that to her.

No matter how much he wanted to.

"I'm sure."

She could keep her old secrets as long as Rhett had the hope of her future.

Chapter Eight

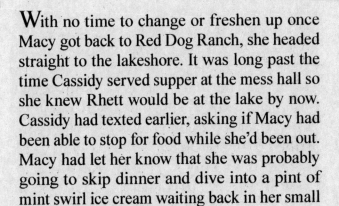

With no time to change or freshen up once Macy got back to Red Dog Ranch, she headed straight to the lakeshore. It was long past the time Cassidy served supper at the mess hall so she knew Rhett would be at the lake by now. Cassidy had texted earlier, asking if Macy had been able to stop for food while she'd been out. Macy had let her know that she was probably going to skip dinner and dive into a pint of mint swirl ice cream waiting back in her small fridge later tonight instead.

Romeo brayed as she passed his enclosure.

"Sorry, buddy, I got nothing. I didn't even get a chance to grab myself food." She reached over the fence and scratched between his ears. He brayed again. "Oh, you impatient little guy, good thing you're so cute. I see you already forgot about the pear chunks I brought you yesterday." Her stomach rumbled.

She left Romeo and continued in the direction of the lake. She hiked up the last hill and paused at the top. Rhett's back was to her as he stood at the end of the long wooden pier with a bundle or some sort of basket by his feet. Kodiak swam after her red ball in the water. A trail of candles burning inside glass jars led the way down the pier to him. The sight caused Macy's pulse to kick up.

Was this…was this a date?

She brushed the thought away. After all, she had been the one to ask him to meet up to talk, not the other way around. Although it was hardly as if Rhett would have set out the candles if he was going to be here alone.

She would not read too much into the gesture.

She would not.

Hopefully, she would believe the statement the more she repeated it to herself.

Kodiak, who had been dropping the ball onto the pier for Rhett to toss out again, swam past the pier to the shore. The dog leapt from the water, gave one great shake and then charged in Macy's direction.

Rhett followed his dog's progress but stayed

on the pier. A wide, handsome smile spread across his features as he slipped his hands into his pockets. "See. What did I tell you? She likes you more than me already."

"Hardly," Macy called back with a laugh.

The dog happily head butted Macy's knee and Macy gave her a welcoming pat only to discover that Kodiak felt dry. "How is this dog not wet?" She touched her coarse fur again.

"Double coated," Rhett answered. "Thick underlayer keeps her skin from ever getting wet. The top layer is considered a harsh coat. You know how a duck can go in the water and comes out without being waterlogged?"

Kodiak trailed along beside Macy as she made her way to the pier. "Don't ducks have some special oil though?"

"Chessies have oil trapped between the two layers of their coat. Works the same way."

Closer to the shore Macy accepted the red ball and threw it out into the lake for Kodiak to go after. Rhett's dog had the endurance of a triathlete.

Rhett came to where the planks connected with the shore and offered his hand. "I have something for you," he said almost shyly.

Macy unsuccessfully fought a wary grin

as she slipped her hand into his. "What is all this?"

Rhett led her to the end of the pier. "Cassidy told me you were planning to skip supper tonight. She gave me the candles." He gave a nervous shrug.

Cassidy. Of course. Always trying to set them up. It was too bad the romantic ambiance hadn't been Rhett's idea, but Macy would enjoy it nonetheless.

The pier creaked and swayed with their steps. Macy noticed each jar had been filled a third of the way with sand before a votive was placed inside. Flames flickered as they passed by, giving the pier a dreamlike quality. Fireflies drawn to the lights whizzed around their legs. Croaking frogs, the lake lapping the underside of the boards, their steps and the slight crunch of the tethered canoe against the side of the pier were the only sounds.

Well, besides Kodiak's feverish paddling.

When they reached the end Rhett let go of her hand so he could tug a blanket from the large tote bucket he must have stowed there. He spread the blanket out then looked over at her, turned and looked out at the lake, cleared his throat, scratched the back of his neck.

Was he…goodness, the man was all nerves.

She, of all people, had flustered Rhett Jarrett. Her logical, straight-talking friend couldn't find words. The realization warmed Macy's heart.

"Rhett," she said his name tenderly. "What is all this?"

He cleared his throat again. "Food." He pulled the top off of the tote bucket. "You weren't at the mess hall so I assumed you hadn't eaten. And Cassidy said she didn't think you had and helped me gather some things. I shouldn't just assume that if you're not with us you're not anywhere though, right? You could have been out on a date instead for all I know." He looked right at her, his blue eyes wider than usual. "Were you on a date? Wait." He held up a hand. "Not my business. You don't have to tell me. Unless you want to, that is. If you do, you can."

Macy pressed her hand over his mouth to stop his rambling. Nervous Rhett was by far the most adorable version of Rhett she had ever encountered.

"Cassidy was right. I have not eaten." And at past eight at night she was definitely hungry now. Macy slowly removed her fingers from his lips. Blood thrummed through her veins at a turbulent pace, making her skin feel tingly. "And I wasn't on a date."

She caught the grin he attempted to hide when he ducked back toward the tote to pull out food. "We had a bad start when I came back. I want to start over like two old friends should have." He handed her a small bundle. "Blue-cheese steak wrap."

"My favorite. You remembered?" Macy took a seat on the blanket facing the lake. She unrolled the parchment paper so she could take a bite of the wrap. The bold notes of blue cheese, spinach and freshly grilled steak made her taste buds dance.

"Of course." Rhett produced a glass bowl full of frozen blueberries—a favorite childhood treat. His mom used to sprinkle them over ice cream or hand out bowls of frozen blueberries on hot summer nights while everyone gathered on the back porch to watch the sunset. Next came a thermos and two cups.

"Just Cassidy's sparkling watermelon lemonade."

"*Just* is not the right word." Macy unscrewed the lid and inhaled the sweet scent emanating from the thermos. "She hasn't made this stuff since last summer and I love it. How did you talk her into it?"

Rhett winked. "I have my ways." His bravado fell to sudden nervousness again. "Okay, and these might not be great, but…" He pulled a small tin from the basket.

When he opened the lid, Macy gasped. "S'mores stuffed cookies. You convinced someone to make them? I haven't had these since…" She snagged one from the tin and sank her teeth into it, letting her eyes flutter closed as the perfect balance of chocolate, marshmallow, graham-cracker crumbs and cookie melted on her tongue. "I think it's been at least ten years since I've had one and they're just as good as I remember."

"Oh, good." Rhett rubbed the back of his neck. "Because I made them and I wasn't sure how they would turn out."

Macy's eyes filled with irrational tears. She had to rapid-fire blink to keep them from falling. "You made these? You got the ingredients and mixed them and cooked them…for me?"

His head dipped with acknowledgment. "Your mom's recipe."

"Thank you," she whispered. She wanted to hug him, to kiss him and to cry too. The last time Macy had tasted these cookies her mom had made them. Each time she had unearthed her mom's spiral notebook full of recipes she had started crying, never able to actually make any of the recipes inside. Besides, she wasn't much of a cook or baker to begin with.

Rhett's gesture was an act of love. Plain and simple.

This was the man she had lost her heart to so many years ago.

Rhett hung his legs over the edge of the pier while Macy finished eating. He scuffed his palms along the thighs of his jeans, trying to will them to stop sweating. A lot of good that did.

Macy gently set the tin of cookies down and scooted to sit beside him at the end of the pier. "Tonight… This is…this is so beautiful, Rhett. What you did for me."

I did it because I love you. I'd do this every day if it made you happy. I should have done this a long time ago.

His throat burned with words he had to swallow.

Tonight wasn't the time to declare anything. Tonight was an olive branch, letting her know he was serious about them being friends again.

A candle flickered in the breeze beside him. Cassidy had forced him to bring those along and had even sent a kitchen hand to set it all up. He thought the candles were a bit much for renewing friendship, but he knew better than to argue with Cassidy when her mind was made up.

He braced his hands at an angle so one was behind her, bringing them even closer. Raven strands of her hair danced in the breeze, the long ends traced across his shoulder.

"That day, when I left the ranch…" The words were out before he could consider them.

She scooped her hair to the side and turned toward him so their faces were less than a foot apart. Waning sunlight backlit her and his breath caught for a moment. She was the most beautiful person he had ever seen. She licked her lips, drawing his attention to how much he wanted to kiss her.

He sat up, pulling away from her a bit in the process. She mirrored his posture, leaning forward now so her shoulder bumped his arm.

"You stopped me, on my way out." An image of Macy with tears streaking down her cheeks played in his mind, unbidden. It tore at his heart.

"I was afraid you were going to leave without saying goodbye."

On that day he *had* planned to leave the ranch without saying goodbye to anyone. He had been so angry after his father's ultimatum—stay and stop questioning Brock's methods or leave for good.

He rubbed his hands together slowly. If only it was so easy to dust off mistakes. "You told me I was wrong. You said I had to see my dad's side," he said. "All I heard was you choosing him, choosing this place over me like he'd done so many times."

"When you said it was you or the ranch, I didn't know how to answer," Macy admitted. "I loved your dad as if he was my father. Your family had become mine. I didn't just want to leave everything. My home. When you offered me the job on the spot, it came out of nowhere."

He turned his head her way again. Had to see her eyes. "There was more to it than that. I… I wanted you to pick me. I wanted someone—wanted you—to choose me." For his entire life, his dad had never picked him. Rhett had never felt as if he was first place in anyone's heart. He had wanted to be the top person in Macy's life that day, but he knew it had been wrong to demand she choose him over everything else. He couldn't hold the eye contact—not after that admission—so he gazed out at the lake. "You had been dating that guy."

"Jim." She scooted closer.

"Yeah, him."

She surprised Rhett by laying her head on his shoulder. "I'm tired. Do you mind?"

Rhett fought the urge to turn his nose into her hair and breathe in her scent. "Not at all."

"Jim didn't like you." She adjusted where her head was, nestling even closer. She sighed. "He told me to stop spending so much time with you and I did."

"I noticed." Rhett slipped off his hat and set it beside him. Then he leaned his head to rest it on hers. They had never been like this before, so easy with their physical contact, but it felt right. It made Rhett wonder why he had never put his arm around her or reached out for her before now. "And I didn't like it."

"You were jealous?"

"Practically bursting with it," he said. He swallowed hard. "Then after you showed up and turned down the job…" He omitted the kiss after how the conversation had gone last night. "Then you wouldn't return my calls. It seemed I had successfully run off the one person who had always been in my corner, so I figured I was meant to be alone. Later, when you called—" he heaved a sigh "—I convinced myself you were better off without me."

Macy sat up suddenly and scooted so she was half facing him. She dropped her hand to his knee. "We may be the two stupidest people on the planet."

"I don't follow."

"That kiss? I wanted to be with you, Rhett." She looked away. "I had wanted that for a long time. When things didn't go well… I was horrified, to say the least."

"Mace." He couldn't let her continue to believe he hadn't wanted her. Hadn't imagined that kiss differently a million times over the last three years. "I was surprised. But it was a good surprised," he rushed on. "And I muddled it completely."

"You kept saying, 'Why did you do that?'"

He had only meant to start the conversation.

"It all happened so fast." But it had definitely been the wrong thing to say. However, he had pushed back his feelings for Macy for so long and hadn't allowed himself to entertain the idea that maybe she cared deeply for him, as well.

"When I finally worked up the nerve to call back and you never responded, I assumed it was because you didn't want me. Your messages had just said that we needed to talk so I had no clue if it was a good talk or a bad talk. This whole time I've been telling myself something was missing, something was—" her voice caught "—wrong with me. First my dad, then you." She swiped at her eyes.

Heaviness settled on Rhett's chest and lungs as she spoke. He'd had a hand in causing these insecurities. Aware of them now, he would fight them alongside of her for the rest of their lives in whatever capacity she would allow him to.

"Mace." He caught her face between his hands. "There has never been, nor will there ever be, anything you can do or say that will make me not want you in my life. My pride kept me away—that's on me and only me. You are perfect the way you are and I'd never want you to change. That was a lot of words, but I mean it. You have been my closest friend— my best friend—for most of my life. I'd like to erase everything that happened between us ever since I left and just go back to how we were for so many years."

Macy shrugged from his touch.

"Go back to how we were," she said robotically. "Of course. Friends." Her smile didn't reach her eyes.

"It's getting late. Is it okay if I share the thing I wanted to talk about now?"

His hands dropped away from her. During his spur-of-the-moment conversation he had lost track of the fact that she had been the one who wanted to talk about something. "I bulldozed this whole night, didn't I?"

"I didn't mind. We needed to hash this stuff out."

His hat still off, Rhett ran his hand through his hair. "Please, what was it you wanted to talk about?"

Macy grimaced. "It's business stuff—but I'm really excited."

He grabbed his hat and set it back on his head. "Bring it on."

"Let's clean as we talk." She motioned toward the basket. Macy started gathering plates and other items and handing them his way to stow in the bucket he had brought. Rhett got up and started gathering the candles.

The sun had finished its dip to the other side of the world and the fields had turned dark. Kodiak lay a few feet away, catching a small nap. If the three of them could have stayed like this then life would have been perfect. Too bad reality knocked hard enough to wake the heaviest dreamer.

They had made their peace, but Rhett still had to make amends with Shannon and chart the best path for the ranch going forward. Running Camp Firefly was a full-time job on its own, and summer was the busiest time with the cattle. On top of that he still had to replace some essential staff members who had left after his father passed. Soon enough Rhett would have to start putting in fourteen-hour workdays just to keep up.

Maybe things would settle down by the time autumn rolled around.

Macy handed him the blanket. "I might have messaged someone about the egg hunt and not told you about it."

He chuckled. The worry in her voice was evident and he wanted to put her at ease.

"So now you have to tell me, huh?"

She rose and grabbed both his hands, giving them one quick pump as she said, "It's Clint Oakfield."

"*The* Clint Oakfield?" Rhett knew he was bound to be gaping but he couldn't help it. The man had recently been inducted into the Grand Ole Opry.

"The one and only. He wants to come to our event and he's bringing all kinds of signed merch to raffle off. He's also made a donation that covers more than half of our expenses. If it's okay with you, of course. He wants to do a few songs and—"

Rhett caught her up in a hug, lifting her clear off the ground. "You're amazing! You know that, right?"

Kodiak bounded to her feet and came over to them, tail wagging, as she picked up on their excitement. When Rhett set Macy down she turned to lavish attention on Kodiak, and he found he was glad for the distraction.

Because without Kodiak's interruption he very well might have kissed Macy and ruined all the steps they had taken toward mending their friendship tonight.

Chapter Nine

The day of the egg hunt had dawned with an overwhelming cloak of muggy air descending onto the ranch. Macy pulled her hair into a ponytail and fanned her face. With all the running around involved for setup and directing others, she was already on her second shirt of the day and was considering changing again or at least freshening up before the candy drop occurred.

She glanced at her watch. There wouldn't be enough time.

Thankfully no one seemed to be letting the unseasonably warm, damp weather affect their attitudes, nor had it negatively impacted the turnout. Kids and guardians swarmed every inch of Red Dog Ranch. The sight of all of them smiling and enjoying their day filled Macy's heart to the point of bursting.

Every fight, every miscommunication, every late night had been worth it.

The staff and interns had cleared out the largest field in preparation for the candy drop and local businesses had banded together to set up a carnival complete with games, prizes, snacks, horse rides and a petting zoo on the opposite side of the driveway. The little goats included in the petting zoo were the talkative type, filling the air with their bleats. Buses lined the fenced area in the overflow parking section. Clint Oakfield was stationed near the mess hall for photos and signatures, and Jack Donnelley had the helicopter parked near Sheep and Romeo's enclosure. The helicopter was open so kids could go inside, pretend they were flying it and have their pictures taken. A tent nearby served as a place where kids could paint eggs to take home.

Macy decided it was the most successful Easter event the ranch had ever hosted. Wistfully she wished Brock had lived to see this day. He would have been so proud of Rhett, proud of her too.

A sudden stiff wind tore down through the row of hills lining their property, sending some of the promotional signs flying. Macy jogged after them, gathering up the mess.

"Here's another one." A man in a red shirt handed her one she must have missed.

Macy thanked him and stowed the rest inside the Jarrett house, using the diversion as an excuse to also check on Mrs. Jarrett. Rhett's mom observed the event through the floor-to-ceiling, two-story-high windows in the comfort of her living room. For as long as Macy had known the woman, she had been this way—watchful, perceptive and thoughtful. Alzheimer's might have stolen her ability to make new memories or to recall what year she was currently in, but it hadn't taken the truest things about her. Not yet.

"Ah, there's our dear lady." A smile bloomed on Mrs. Jarrett's face when she spotted Macy. "Looks like a good turnout despite the forecast."

"Everything is going really well," Macy assured her. "Last I heard, it's not supposed to storm until later."

Mrs. Jarrett gestured toward the large bank of windows. "I know we have you to thank for this day. And don't tell me this was Rhett's doing because I know you've worked so hard, dear. I'm so proud of you." She reached out her hand.

Macy grasped it. "You're too kind. You always know how to bless me with the right words."

"Bless you? Oh, child, you're the one who has always been a blessing to this family. Not the other way around, Macy Howell. You are our blessing. I want you to remember that." ·

You are our blessing. ·

Could it be true? Macy had never considered herself a blessing to anyone. A burden. Forgettable. Not enough.

Never a blessing.

But Mrs. Jarrett was not one to say anything carelessly.

"Send Brock inside if it gets bad, will you?" Mrs. Jarrett twisted toward the windows again. She drew a blanket around her shoulders. "His joints are probably already barking at him. All this moisture will do that."

Macy urged the nurse on duty to make sure Mrs. Jarrett had extra opportunities to rest today as all the additional people and excitement could make for a rough night for the older woman.

With the knowledge that Mrs. Jarrett was in great hands, Macy headed back outside and surveyed the party from the large wraparound porch. She rested her hand on the walkie-talkie and considered calling Rhett, but she knew he was busy giving tours of the camper cabins to local businessmen who had expressed interest in potentially partnering with Camp Firefly. He was exactly where he needed to be and she wouldn't distract him.

No matter how badly she wanted to.

The weeks leading up to the event had blurred together in a whirl of planning, running errands and scheduling. Rhett had thrown himself into helping and had even called in favors from past dog-training clients, all of which had made a huge difference. Through his connections the price of the food had been covered, among other things. On top of that, the man had spent every weekend working on last-minute maintenance throughout the ranch, but especially devoting extra time and attention toward getting the camper cabins ready for the summer. Time and again she had stopped by on a Saturday to find him knee-deep in manual labor, sleeves rolled up and covered in sweat…handsomer than ever.

It had warmed Macy's heart to see Rhett finally stepping up to help with the foster programs offered at Red Dog Ranch. He went about it in a different way than his father had, but honestly, Rhett had a better mind for the big picture when it came to planning. Macy had come to really appreciate his input and insight. She had come to rely on him.

Not only that but he had started seeing his dog-training clients again. Only a few for now, but it was progress. She had left information about courses for people who wanted to train therapy dogs on his desk and he had promised to sign up for something in the fall.

While she had loved finally being able to work toward a common goal with him, side by side, and while it had been exhilarating and encouraging striving in tandem to make the event a success in such a short amount of time, Macy couldn't help the lingering feeling of disappointment that occasionally tiptoed into her heart.

What had happened to the romantic man she had enjoyed supper with on the pier weeks ago? Perhaps she had misinterpreted everything that evening, but whenever she replayed it—his warm gazes and tender words, his kind gestures like the cookies—she found herself bewildered all over again.

Despite his many mentions of the word *friend*, that night she had wanted him to kiss her. More than she ever had before. But he hadn't. Even after they left the pier, Rhett had insisted on walking her to her bungalow and she was sure he had a reason other than her safety. It wasn't as if she hadn't walked alone on the ranch's property a million other times. But he had strolled beside her all the way to the pebbled path leading to her bungalow, wished her good-night and walked away.

In the following days she had expected him to offer some sort of clarification, but it seemed that Rhett had clammed up again, at least where she was concerned. Oh, he had completely gone all out helping with the egg hunt and had begun intentionally mentoring Gabe, as well. He was talking about hiring some of the interns on for the summer. Rhett had risen to the occasion. Macy had no complaints there.

But it left her wondering...

He felt something for her, something more than friendship. No one could have convinced Macy otherwise, but something was holding him back.

Jack flagged Macy down. "We're going to move up the candy drop. I don't like the looks of that." He pointed to the black clouds piling up in the distance. "Rhett okayed it, but he said to check with you."

Macy radioed to Cassidy. "How are the hams? About done?"

Her walkie-talkie crackled a second later. "We can plate as soon as twenty minutes."

Macy nodded and Jack jogged toward his helicopter. The interns helped direct the crowd to line up near the marked off portions of the large field and Macy followed in their wake. As was tradition, Rhett's uncle Travis took the stage to rattle off instructions.

The helicopter lifted off, beating the air in huge waves. Macy shivered, but the children cheered. Jack circled the field once, allowing the rest of his onboard crew to get into position along the open sides of the large craft. When Travis sounded the bullhorn the helicopter crew began dropping candy out of the helicopter until the field was colorful with it.

Although raindrops weren't falling at the ranch yet, the sky just beyond their property had turned pitch-black with rain. A storm would rip through Red Dog Ranch within minutes. As Jack's helicopter left the area kids were allowed to converge on the field to fill their bags. Macy wanted to urge everyone to go quickly, but the kids hardly needed to be told.

Macy ran toward Romeo and Sheep's enclosure. "I know neither of you appreciate getting rained on." She attached lead lines to both of their halters and walked them toward the barn. Halfway there, Romeo pinned his ears back and started braying. He planted his hoofs.

"Come on, you goof." Macy tried to coax him with a promise of a treat later. "Let's get you inside and everything will be fine." But the tiny donkey balked.

Rhett appeared beside her, his brow creased with worry. "This storm is bearing down quicker than they predicted." His head swiveled in the direction of the approaching storm. "It looks like a wall of clouds. I can't say I've ever seen anything like it."

Macy tossed the lead lines over her shoulder to free up her hands. She grabbed both animals' halters and used the leverage of all her weight to lean in the opposite direction. "We just need to get people inside."

Rhett pushed Romeo's rear end, getting the donkey moving again. "I'll send everyone to the mess hall."

"You deal with the people and I'll get everything else stowed away," she called after him as he headed to the stage.

Kodiak took off after Rhett, but suddenly

stopped and looked back at Macy. She whimpered low in her throat.

Rhett glanced back. "Stay with Macy."

Kodiak charged to join her as Macy fumbled with the lock on the barn.

Rain began to ping off the roofs, the dirt. One second it was sprinkling and before she could open the barn door it was pouring down. Cold water trickled down her spine and her legs.

As she secured Sheep and Romeo in their stalls she heard Rhett on the loudspeakers directing people toward the mess hall. A heartbeat later, a loud crash of thunder had Romeo bucking in his stall. Macy hoped someone had seen to the group of horses that were being used for rides.

Kodiak pressed close to Macy's legs.

"You can stay in here, girl." Macy ran her fingers over the dog's coarse fur. "You'll be safe and dry and don't need to worry about me." Macy made for the door and Kodiak matched her step for step.

"I said stay." Macy made her voice commanding.

Kodiak barked and followed Macy as she plucked one of the shared heavy-duty raincoats from a peg on the wall and made her way outside.

Macy looked down at the dog beside her. "You're just as stubborn as your master, aren't you?"

Kodiak met her eyes and barked again. Her last command from Rhett would be followed to the letter, no matter what Macy told the dog.

Macy tugged the hood of her coat up. "Well, come on then. We've got work to do."

"It's warm inside. And smell that?" Rhett sniffed the air for the benefit of the scared, young kids filing past him. "Nobody makes ham like our cook, Miss Cassidy. And if I were you, I'd snag an extra one of her ched-dar-cheese rolls. Believe me." Rhett held the mess hall's front door open until the last person had entered.

Due to the storm, many people had opted to get on the road instead of stay for the meal the ranch always hosted as a fund-raiser after-ward. Rhett couldn't blame them for heading out. He prayed they all made it to their desti-nations safely. It looked as if it was going to be one wicked storm.

He secured the door then shook rain off of his hat. Outside the sky was as dark as midnight despite it only being four in the afternoon. Bright veins of lightning spliced through the black. They lighted up the grounds below the hills for a heartbeat. Rhett frantically scanned the area through the windows along the front porch of the mess hall, looking for any families that might still be out there, but the main fields where they'd held the event were deserted.

The rumble that followed the lightning was immediate and powerful. Inside the mess hall younger kids screamed and ducked their heads under tables.

Rhett lingered in the entryway with his hat still clutched in his hands, waiting for Macy and Kodiak. He wasn't even going to deny that fact. He was fully aware that Macy was smart and capable and did not need him fretting over her because of a thunderstorm.

Yet here he was.

He wouldn't be able to relax until he saw her safe inside.

Rain pelted the building hard. It was as if someone was heaving bucket after bucket of water against their windows. The south pasture near the lake would flood. It always did during bad storms. Thankfully, rain of this magnitude was a rarity. And they had moved the cattle to a different field to get them away from the event, so that wouldn't be an issue.

Wind bent smaller trees sideways. There would be plenty of shingles to fix tomorrow.

Rhett paced the small area and worked his hat around and around in his hands a few times before he remembered his cell phone. Because of dog training, he was in the habit of keeping the contraption on silent. What if Macy had tried to call? What if she needed him? She had warned him to turn the thing on occasionally.

He tugged his phone from his pocket and his heart leapt when he saw one missed call and a voice mail. He thumbed the screen to unlock it. One missed call from Hank, his lawyer friend, who had started booking training sessions for Riptide again. Hank had already told him that the will was as ironclad as they had originally believed, but Rhett didn't care any longer.

Uncle Travis popped his head into the entryway hallway. "You're needed."

Rhett stopped pacing. "Have you seen Macy or Shannon?" His sister was usually actively involved during events, but he hadn't seen her all day. Hopefully she was in the house with their mom.

His uncle gave Rhett a thoughtful look. "I saw Macy on my way in. She said she was going to gather as much of the setup stuff as she could before the worst of the storm rolled in. Good thing too. Stuff from the games would have ended up all over the ranch with this wind."

Rhett headed toward the door. "She shouldn't be out there alone. I should be helping her."

His uncle snagged his arm. When Rhett looked back to argue, Travis jerked his head toward the speaker system set up at the front of the mess hall. "This shindig always starts with a word from the owner and a prayer. It's tradition."

"But—"

"Macy is a grown woman who knows what she can handle. You're the owner. These people are your responsibility. You are needed here." Uncle Travis ushered Rhett away from the doorway. "I'll try to get in touch with Shannon if that would ease your mind."

Rhett nodded and tucked his phone away, but he glanced through the front windows one last time. Macy was out there and so was Kodiak. *Keep them safe, Lord. Please watch over them.*

When Rhett stepped into the dining area, a hush fell over the crowd. He dipped his head as he walked. Rhett made eye contact with a few of the children on his way to the front of the room. One little boy flashed him a thumbs-up so Rhett returned the gesture and added a wink for good measure.

The aroma of freshly baked rolls and chocolate cake along with ham and caramelized pineapple drifted through the room. Rhett's mouth watered. Cassidy and her crew of volunteers had spent all day in the kitchen working on the feast. He couldn't wait to taste everything.

The speaker system was used primarily during the summer months for making announcements or telling the campers to simmer down on occasion. They hadn't used it recently and Rhett absently hoped it was still functioning. Rhett picked up the microphone and tapped it twice. It worked just fine.

"Good afternoon and thank you for braving the storm for this event," Rhett started. He hadn't planned anything to say. In truth, he had forgotten about the little spiel his dad had always given. Brock's talk had lasted a few minutes, a sermon of sorts. Often it included the salvation message.

Rhett let his focus slowly trip across everyone in the room. So many kids and all of them either waiting for a permanent home or waiting for their homes to become a safe place for them once again. Seeing so many of them in front of him, it tore at his heart. After visiting with them all day and seeing their hopeful faces, now Rhett knew that he wanted to help them to continue to be the legacy of Red Dog Ranch.

No matter what, he would choose these kids. This life. This place.

The legacy not only his dad had secured for him, but God too.

He would figure out a way to keep all the programs, turn a profit at the ranch and still train dogs on the side. With Travis, Macy, Cassidy, Shannon and many others—there were plenty of them to divide the work between. Together they would make it a success.

For the first time in what felt like years, Rhett finally understood his dad's passion and drive and he wanted to lay down all his past hurts to honor all his dad had built.

Rhett blinked against the sudden rush of emotions. "I know many of you must have wondered what would happen to Red Dog Ranch after my father passed." He found Uncle Travis in the room and for a heartbeat he pictured Brock there too, beaming and happy. Though this wasn't for his dad any longer; it was for Rhett. "A wise man once asked me if I knew the heart of God when it came to this place and I'm ashamed to admit I brushed his challenge off. But God has this funny way of not letting us forget something like that."

A loud rumble of thunder shook the building and the lights browned out for a few seconds. People in the crowd murmured worriedly. He needed to keep this short and sweet.

Rhett began to walk between the tables as he spoke. "How do we know the heart of God?"

"The Bible!" a little girl called out.

Rhett pointed her way. "Great answer. The Bible shows us God's heart. And what are we celebrating today?"

"Easter!" This time a chorus of kids joined in.

"That's right, Easter. The greatest showing of God's heart for this world. Our heavenly Father loves us so much that He wanted to make a way for us to never be parted from Him. He loves us enough to sacrifice His son so that we can have a relationship with Him." Rhett headed back to the front of the room. "So back to my friend's question—do I know the heart of God in this matter? Yes, well, yes I do. The heart of God, the answer to every question concerning what I should do—what each of us should do in our lives—is love. In any situation we have to ask ourselves, 'What is the loving thing to do?' Then we have our answer."

Cassidy stood near the pass-through, ready to hand out the food. Rhett caught her wiping a tear away.

"My father left behind a legacy of love and I mean to continue it."

The dining hall erupted with cheers and applause. A man seated nearby got to his feet and threw his arms around Rhett in an awkward hug. Clearly Macy hadn't been the only person worried about how Rhett would run Red Dog Ranch.

"How about we say a prayer and then dig in to this food?" Rhett smiled at the crowd. "It smells amazing."

But before Rhett could bow his head Jack Donnelley slammed open the side door so loudly it caused people at nearby tables to jump out of their seats. Jack rushed toward Rhett with the intensity of a bomb-sniffing dog on patrol.

Jack reached Rhett, phone in hand. "My dispatch center just called. Tornado warning. It's touched down less than a mile away. It could be on us in minutes, maybe less." Jack's police training showed as he calmly delivered the information. "We need to get people to safety."

Hands shaking, Rhett got back on the microphone. "Change of plans. We're under a tornado warning. I need everyone to proceed in a single-file line down to the basement."

A few people yelled and more started to cry, but everyone got to their feet quickly and headed toward one of the sets of stairs. Thankfully, there were plenty of adults to help guide the children. Jack, Uncle Travis and Rhett each manned the top of one of the three entrances to the basement, directing people to go down and as far back as they could.

Rhett sent Macy a text:

Tornado. Get inside.

He almost typed I love you but wasn't that something that should be said first instead of texted? He loved Macy. The last few weeks had cemented that truth and thinking of her outside in the storm… All the roadblocks he had imagined between them suddenly felt insignificant. He had made peace with his father and let go of his pain and had done all he could to care for his mother. Besides, if he waited to act on his feelings until everything in his life was perfect the time would never come.

Fear had made excuses easy to believe, but he refused to chart his steps by fear any longer. Next time he saw her he would tell her how he felt. She might reject him, but he would deal with it if she did.

But a text stole some of the power away from declaring love. Then again, what if he never got the chance to tell her? What if...

He refused to think like that.

Cassidy had immediately whisked Piper to the basement and Rhett could hear her instructing people to get on their knees and cover their necks.

Keep people safe, Lord. Please protect all these people.

Maybe the tornado would miss the ranch. Maybe it would change course.

The building started to rattle under an onslaught of wind. Rhett instructed people to head down the steps a little quicker. They were almost done. Almost everyone now.

With his phone in his hand, Rhett willed Macy to call him. To tell him she was fine, tucked away somewhere safe. But he couldn't think only of her either. Other people depended on him. Rhett pulled up the number for the phone his mother's on-duty nurse carried and hit Call.

He didn't even let her greet him. "A tornado's touched down. It's close. Get to the lower interior bathroom. Put Mom in the tub. Grab pillows, blankets—anything to protect yourselves. Stay in there until one of us comes to get you guys."

"Understood." The nurse hung up.

Rhett's mind raced. His ears popped, more painfully than on any flight he had ever been on. The deep sink he was standing near gurgled and then the drain made one long, desperate suctioning sound. Rhett hurtled down the steps to join the others in the basement.

While Northern Texas experienced a fair amount of tornados, they were far less common in the hill country. And with Red Dog Ranch so far away from any of the local towns, he had never even heard a siren before and it wasn't as if they had their own alert system.

Tornados happened, but in thirty years Rhett had never seen one, never been in one.

The deafening howl outside told him that was about to change.

Chapter Ten

Even though she was wearing a heavy coat the rain started to pelt Macy so hard it physically hurt to be outside anymore. And it was cold. Horribly, painfully cold now.

The rain suddenly switched to falling sideways. Dime-sized hail clanged on a nearby roof, coming closer, peppering the ground.

Macy's teeth rattled and her legs trembled as she made her way through a patch of mud. She would catch a cold from this adventure; there was zero doubt in her mind about that. She should have headed inside ten minutes ago—should have gone in with everyone else instead of trying to be useful.

Macy turned to head toward the barn. It was a smelly place to ride out the weather, but it was near and would provide adequate shelter from the wind and wetness. A pole barn full of machinery and the Jarretts' ranch house were also within proximity, but both were farther than the solid oak barn where Romeo, Sheep and the other horses were kept.

When hail was part of the equation, Macy would choose close over comfort.

However, she couldn't make out the barn any longer. Darkness disoriented her. It was as if her eyes were closed. Macy pivoted a full 360 degrees, scanning the area, squinting, but it was no use. She couldn't even tell if she was facing in the correct direction any longer.

Dread pooled like a cooling ball of lead in the pit of her stomach. Weighty. Impossible to escape.

Kodiak rubbed against her leg and Macy steadied herself with a hand on the dog's shoulder. Kodiak's body shuddered under her fingers. Macy winced as her ears suddenly popped with an excruciating and sudden change in pressure.

Then she heard it.

A roar.

The sound of a train engine but louder. It vibrated through her whole body, her bones.

Tornado.

The wall of rain clouds had hidden a tornado.

An angry churning funnel headed directly toward the barn Macy had wanted to seek shelter in only moments ago. If the tornado stayed its course the horse barn would take a direct hit. The rest of the horses were in the pasture so they had the ability to get out of the way, but Sheep and Romeo were inside the building. And there was no time to set them loose; she wouldn't be able to make it. Macy's heart slammed into the back of her throat and sickness washed over her. If something happened to them, she had put them in there. She would be at fault.

But she couldn't think about that right now. Macy had to get to safety.

Go. Move. Get out of here.

A tiny piece of debris slammed into Macy's arm and she cried out as if she had been shot. Warmth seeped over the area. Hot and burning. Blood.

Macy grabbed for Kodiak's collar and yanked her toward the ranch house. "Run! We have to run."

She took off toward the house, knowing Rhett's faithful dog would stick close. She could do this. She could protect them. She could beat this storm.

Faster. Go. Faster.

Her legs burned. She slipped in deep mud and fell onto all fours. Her hands suctioned into the mire. Kodiak shoved her head under Macy's chest as if the dog was trying to lift her up. Macy scrambled forward on all fours, trying to get purchase.

Winds ripped a long swatch of fencing up out of the ground with a sickening crunch and tossed it in a tangled heap only yards away. A huge old tree snapped and took flight.

Wood from the horse barn began to splinter. The barn walls buckled and heaved behind her. Macy looked back to see the roof fly off and go up into the sky as if it weighed nothing. Gone.

Gathering additional debris, the funnel grew darker, larger. Its furious howl filled her ears until it was all she could hear, all she could think about.

She found her feet again and started for the ranch house. If she ran fast enough, she could still make it. She could skid inside and go under the huge, heavy table in their formal dining room. The room had no windows and sat almost in the center of the home, next to their interior bathroom where hopefully Rhett's mom was by now.

Macy was close enough. She would make it.

Everything would be okay. It had to be. God hadn't brought them this far just to—

Kodiak's high-pitched yelp brought Macy up short. She whirled around to see Rhett's dog on the ground ten feet behind her with a large sheet of metal pinning her back half to the ground. Kodiak's front paws dug forward in an effort to pull herself out, but it was no use. Kodiak collapsed, her yellow eyes seeking out Macy.

If Macy kept moving she could make it to shelter in time, but she would have to leave Rhett's dog behind.

Not going to happen.

Macy plunged back toward the storm. Stiff winds sent rocks and other debris hurtling around her. Something scraped the side of her face. She pressed on. She dropped to her knees beside Kodiak. "It's okay, girl." Macy wrapped her fingers around the edge of the sheet of roofing. "I won't leave you."

She heaved the piece of metal with all her might. It was heavy and awkward. Her back spasmed, her biceps felt as if they were being shredded and her legs shook. Under normal circumstances Macy couldn't have budged the thing with only her strength. Macy grunted, putting all her weight into it, and was able to lift the debris enough for Kodiak to army crawl out of the opening.

Another loud, nauseating groan and the pole barn shattered like a child's art project constructed out of toothpicks. Large sections crashed onto the ground around them. That building was full of machinery—heavy metal and steel machinery that the tornado would toss around like confetti. Macy threw her body over Kodiak and braced her arms over her own neck and head.

They would never make it to the house now.

Get to the lowest point.

It was the only thing she could remember about tornados. Since all the structures that could protect them were too far away, they had to get over the hill to the lower area near Canoe Landing. Doing so might take them out of the path entirely. Macy hoisted Kodiak to her paws.

"Please be able to stand."

Kodiak had to be sixty to seventy pounds so there was little chance that Macy could carry her too far. The dog limped but kept up with her. They rushed down the hill, skidding and sliding their way down. Macy's arm and cheek stung like fire.

The lake was full of junk the tornado had

tossed around and the shores were littered, as well. Macy grabbed a large piece of wood that must have been torn from the horse barn and wedged it up so they could get into the ditch under it. At least the board would deflect smaller debris. She reached back and hauled Kodiak to the lowest point, this ditch that fed into the lake, just as the winds increased and the funnel twitched toward them. Macy wiggled into the small space so she was lying across Rhett's dog, then she pulled the wood up over them and prayed.

Kodiak burrowed her muzzle into Macy's neck so her nose was beside Macy's ear. The noise of the dog's steady breathing mixed with the sounds of destruction above them. Macy braced her arms tighter over their heads and slammed her eyes shut as if that would help.

"I'm here, sweet girl," Macy whispered.

Was this it? After everything, was this how her life ended?

Facing the possibility of death, Macy's mind raced back through twenty-eight years of life. Her father leaving, her mother's death, being all alone at only eighteen. The last ten years living with the Jarretts and her friendship with Rhett. The work she had done at the ranch and the lives she had come into contact with because of Brock's mission. Late nights spent giggling with Shannon and Cassidy. Quiet moments with Mrs. Jarrett.

Her evening on the pier with Rhett.

Macy had never felt truly loved and accepted in her life. She had always believed there was something defective about her. Some reason why no one wanted to commit. Why no one stayed.

But…it had always been a lie, hadn't it?

You're the one who has always been a blessing to this family. Not the other way around, Macy Howell. You are our blessing.

The Jarretts had welcomed and loved her as is. Shannon and Cassidy had become sisters to her. Macy had a place to belong—people who would miss her and mourn for her if this was her end. They hadn't loved her for all the late nights she'd spent in the office or the weekends she'd pitched in with the animals or the programs she had helped launch. It hadn't mattered what she had done or accomplished.

They had just loved…her.

Macy had always been enough, just as she was.

Tears stung her eyes; they leaked onto Kodiak's fur.

She had treated God the same way, hadn't

she? Always trying to do enough and accomplish more so she would feel as if she deserved His love.

What an absurd way to live. She had no more power or ability to earn God's love than she had to stop this tornado. The might of the terrible tornado paled in comparison to an almighty God—and He loved her. He had sent His son to die for her.

"Forgive me," she whispered. "I love You. Thank You for loving me. If…if this is when I meet You, I'm ready. Just please take care of all these people. I love them so much. Take care of Rhett."

She prayed the mess hall would be untouched.

Something large slammed into the side of the building and the lights flickered. Someone in the basement wailed uncontrollably.

Seconds after Rhett's boots hit the basement's concrete floor the whole building plunged into darkness. Kids screamed and the soothing voices of many adults followed. Not wanting to step on anyone, Rhett fumbled around. His hand glanced against the doorknob on the door that led to the walk out where trucks made deliveries. It was a sturdy door, but in the end it was only wood.

Not good.

A tornado could wrench that door open and suck people out. He was suddenly very thankful for his dad's foresight in insisting on an unconventional basement being built at the ranch, but the first thing Rhett would do was make this entrance more secure.

If he made it out.

Rhett braced his back against the door as if that might help and then he groped for the lock, found it and slipped it into the locked position. The small bolt probably wouldn't help much, but Rhett was willing to take every measure he had at his disposal to protect all the people gathered at his ranch.

His ranch.

Not his dad's. Not Brock's mission or dreams. Rhett's.

All the glass windows upstairs shattered. It sounded like a series of rapid bombs going off in a war zone. The building started violently shaking and the door behind him vibrated like a jackhammer.

The tornado was passing over them.

Please, Lord, please. I don't care what happens to me but protect these people. Protect Macy and Kodiak and the rest of my family.

Metal rattled and crashed in the kitchen

above them. If there was a person screaming a foot away from him, Rhett wouldn't have been able to tell. He could only hear the storm—there was only the tornado and it was all encompassing.

The walls of the building creaked and popped, moaning under the storm's violent onslaught. Something boomed against the door. It sounded like someone was smacking it with a huge metal chain. The bottom corner peeled back with such sudden force Rhett gasped. Wind lashed in. Just as quickly, tiny debris shoved through the crack in the door frame—nails and wood and a mess of other items—until the small opening was plugged.

Then there was nothing. No wind, no pounding. Rhett could hear his heartbeat reverberating in his ears.

"Is it…" a tentative voice said nearby. "Do we think it's over?"

"Gabe?" Rhett reached toward the voice.

Gabe grabbed his arm. "It's me, Mr. Jarrett."

Rhett yanked the teenage boy into a bear hug. "We're safe. I think it's over." He lifted his head away from Gabe's. "Jack? You nearby?"

Jack's face became illuminated by his phone. "It's dissipated." Jack turned toward the expanse that was the long dark basement.

"It looks like the tornado is done but everyone needs to stay put. I know it's uncomfortable in here and not fun to stay with the lights out, but this is the safest place."

Gabe shuffled his feet. "But I thought you said it was all done?"

Jack inclined his head. He fiddled with something on his phone that kept it illuminated. "It is, but the aftermath can be just as dangerous as the storm itself. Downed power lines and sharp objects everywhere. It's not safe to send everyone out yet." He typed into his phone. "EMS is on the way." He turned toward Rhett. "I'm heading out to assess. You're welcome to join me."

Rhett had pulled out his phone but couldn't get a signal. "My phone's not working." There was no message from Macy. No calls from his mom or Shannon.

Jack held up his phone. "Department phone. I'm connected to a different system. Normal cell infrastructures will be bogged down for the next few hours." Jack stepped toward the door. "Are you coming or staying?"

Rhett looked back into the darkness that held all the people who had come to the ranch expecting a fun day. He had a duty to take care of them, but he also needed to check on his mom and he needed to find Macy, Kodiak and Shannon. In the rush Rhett hadn't been able to touch base with Uncle Travis to see if he had made contact with Shannon.

"Found it," broke in a voice and then a flashlight came on. Cassidy held it, with Piper beside her. "Go, Rhett. We'll take care of everyone here."

Clint Oakfield appeared nearby. "She's right." He sent Cassidy a tentative grin. "We'll take it from here. For as long as you need." He clasped Rhett's shoulder. "You go do what you need to do."

Rhett and Jack shouldered the door open and light spilled in. Clint stacked a few milk crates together to form a makeshift bench for him and Cassidy, then as Rhett and Jack left they heard the country entertainer sing the first few notes of "Amazing Grace" while a chorus of voices joined in.

Emotion clogged Rhett's throat as he stepped clear of the mess hall and surveyed the terrible destruction across the ranch below him. The sky was still menacing, gloomy with a thick fog spreading into the lower sections of his land, but he could see plenty clear enough to know that Red Dog Ranch would never be the same again.

There was a mess of splinters where once there was a row of ten camper cabins. Hunks of steel hung from the trees they passed while other trees were shaved down to only gnarly bent trunks. One of their largest tractors lay on its side in what used to be the horse pasture. Where had that thing been parked beforehand? Nowhere near where it rested now. A bus had been tossed into the office building and cars that had been parked along the driveway were totaled—on their roof or sides, all windows blown out, frames twisted into odd angles.

"It's pretty messed up, huh?" Gabe's voice made Rhett whirl around.

"What are you doing here? You should be back in the basement."

Gabe crossed his arms over his chest. "You'll need help finding Miss Macy. I want to help. Besides, Cassidy said I could go with you."

Rhett considered arguing with the teenager but Jack broke in. "Stick close. Don't wander anywhere without either me or Rhett. Understood?"

"Understood." Gabe nodded. "I'll be like a shadow."

Rhett, Gabe and Jack picked their way carefully down the hill, stepping over tree limbs and other materials Rhett couldn't make sense of at the moment.

Seeing his ranch ripped to pieces made Rhett's eyes burn. Both of the barns were completely gone. He had no idea how his animals had fared. Did he still have cattle? Horses? The mess hall was still standing but a portion of the roof was gone. The Jarrett family home looked like it had managed to stay together.

Thank You, God.

Rhett began to move a little faster.

Jack kept pace with him. "I'm so sorry."

Rhett swallowed around the lump in his throat. Once, twice, three times before he could speak. "I, ah, for a long time I really didn't like this place." Hot shame poured through his chest but he pressed on. "My father..."

Jack stopped and set a hand on Rhett's shoulder, pulling Rhett to a stop. "He loved you, but he never said it. His heart was divided between his family and the ranch. I know."

Rhett nodded. "But I love this place." He gazed out over the absolute destruction in front of him. "I love—but I realized it all too late. Why am I always one step behind?"

A theme in his life. Too late to say goodbye

to his father. Too late to stop Wade from taking off and ultimately getting killed.

Would he always be one step behind in his life? Doomed to not realize or appreciate all he had been blessed with? He truly was as bullheaded as people said. Why hadn't he been grateful about his inheritance? Sprung to action immediately to help kids. *Kids.* How had he missed every clue Macy no doubt dropped about her feelings earlier in their relationship?

Jack's even voice broke through his thoughts. "It's never too late. As long as you've got breath, don't let anyone—even your own stubborn self—tell you it's too late." Jack jutted his chin toward the ranch house. "You guys go check on your mom first. I'm going to head down the main road and do my best to clear a path so the emergency vehicles can get as close as possible."

"Should we come help you?" Rhett felt torn. He wanted to do the right thing, but fear for his loved ones was eating at him.

Jack held up his hand. "You worry about your family. I'll deal with this. A crew will be here to help in no time. We'll do all we can to search for survivors and secure your area.

From the looks of it, Red Dog Ranch took the brunt of this storm."

"Thank you, Jack." Rhett owed the man so much more than a thank-you. He owed him an apology too. "I've never been much of a friend to you and I wish—"

Jack shook his head. "No more worries, man. Seriously. Just take care of this place. It means a lot to me."

"Me too," Rhett said and meant it.

Rhett hadn't yet made it to the steps leading up to the porch when the front door pounded open and Shannon jogged out.

"Rhett!" She was down the steps in seconds and launched herself at him. Breath whooshed out of his lungs as he tried to keep his feet and catch her at the same time.

"I'm so sorry." Her body shook with tears. Her blond curls were wild. "If something had happened to you…" She dug her fingers into his shoulders. "If you had… I've been so cruel these past few weeks. We fought and—" her voice broke "—I've been—"

"Hey," he said tenderly and set her back so he could see his sister's face. "I love you, kid. I'm glad you're safe."

Her face twisted and she started crying harder. "I l-love you t-too. I'm sorry for—"

"Shh." He leaned forward, pressing a kiss to her forehead. "All that's forgiven and forgotten. I should have been there for you more than I've been in the past. I will be. That's a promise."

She swiped at her eyes.

"Mom?" Rhett asked.

"She's scared and confused and keeps asking about Dad, but she's fine. The nurse too. We rode it out in the bathroom," Shannon said. Her eyes went wide. "The family room though—the wall of windows is gone and there's a small tree in there. But other than that the house looks okay. Out here?" She groaned.

"Macy and Kodiak?"

Shannon's focus snapped back to him and she shook her head. "Macy wasn't with you?" Her brow scrunched. "I just assumed. They're both always with you."

"They weren't with me." The words hurt.

He should have made Macy come inside. He should have never nodded along when she said she was going to clean up the event. He had unknowingly sent Kodiak into the heart of a storm. If something had happened to either of them because of things, because of material, replaceable stuff...

Jaw involuntarily clenching, Rhett fisted his hands. "I have to find her."

God, let them be alive. Let them be all right. Help me find them.

Chapter Eleven

Macy couldn't tell how much time had passed since the storm had ended, but it had stopped just as suddenly as it had begun. One second the gusts were trying to tear the sheet of wood off of them and the next all was still. Quiet.

She tried to bend to reach the phone tucked into the back pocket of her jeans, but her arms were pinned in front of her body and she couldn't make out the watch on her wrist even though it was inches from her face.

Was it night already? Was anyone looking for them?

A few birds tittered and somewhere nearby a group of cattle bellowed back and forth to one another. Each sound filled Macy with an almost irrational amount of joy because both noises spoke of hope to her. She had witnessed the horse barn and the pole barn being annihilated, but maybe, just maybe, that was the total loss to the ranch. Maybe all of the cattle and horses were fine. Maybe even now Sheep and Romeo were grazing in one of the pastures as if nothing was wrong.

She squeezed her eyes shut. She couldn't think about the little horse and donkey. Couldn't let her mind go there. As long as she was under the board and couldn't see the totality of destruction, she had hope. She needed to cling to it.

However, no matter how hard she tried to be positive, it was almost impossible to chase all her unconstructive thoughts away.

What if no one came to free them because no one else had survived? What if she and Kodiak had lived through the tornado's assault only to be trapped under rubble, unable to get free? What if they survived the tornado but died because they were trapped in the aftermath?

Macy's heartbeat hammered in her neck and her temples. Her head pounded. A few tears escaped from her closely shuttered eyes.

Stop.

Thoughts along those lines would help no one. Least of all her.

Stay calm. Keep a clear head. Just keep breathing.

Macy could wiggle her toes, her feet. It was dark and muggy, but she could breathe. The only thing she couldn't do was lift the piece of wood from off of her and Kodiak. While originally the door-sized plank hadn't been very heavy, debris had obviously piled up on top of them to the point that Macy wasn't strong enough to push the covering up enough for them to shimmy out.

Maybe if she rested a bit?

God, I know You see us. I know You care. Please, be with me and Kodiak. Help us feel like we're not completely alone.

Her whole body ached and her muscles burned. Rain and mud had soaked her clothes, and her hair was completely waterlogged. A tremor worked its way through her body. Something substantial and sharp pressed against her left ankle. Kodiak let out a low whimper right before her warm tongue traced up the side of Macy's face, ending at her ear.

What would she have done without Rhett's dog along for comfort and company? Macy would be far more panicked without the warm fluff of Kodiak beside her.

"We made it." Macy nuzzled the dog. "Now we just have to get out of here."

As if her words had stirred the dog to action, Kodiak started wiggling. In an effort to get up, the dog's paw came up and scratched down Macy's arm.

"Ouch. Settle down," Macy commanded her. "You did so well. Just a little longer."

But Kodiak tried to switch positions again. She let out a series of whines and then barked. Macy hushed her, but Rhett's dog continued barking loudly. Her hot breath made the already cramped space feel tight and damp. Macy was about to tell the dog to zip it again when a noise above them caused her to still. Items were being moved. Things were shifting off of their board.

Someone was up there.

"Macy!" Rhett yelled and the desperation in his voice made Macy's heart twist. "Mace, are you there? Dear Lord, please let her be okay. Let me find her. Let her be here."

Macy tried to say something, but her voice was so raw there was no way he heard her. She cleared her throat, trying again. "I'm here. Help! We're under here."

"Thank You, God." Rhett sounded close to tears. "You can breathe? You're all right?"

"I think so."

"Don't move. Let us lift the worst of this away." More stuff shifted above them. "I'm here, Mace. I won't leave until I leave with you in my arms. You have my word."

Kodiak barked frantically again.

Macy grew antsy. Now that she knew rescue was close she felt like she wanted to crawl out of her skin. She didn't want to wait. Couldn't wait. She was too closed in. She wanted to shove the board off of them and never see this ditch again. But she knew Rhett was right. She had no idea what kind of mess was piled above them. There could be live wires for all she knew. There could be a car precariously balanced over them.

I won't leave until I leave with you in my arms.

After what seemed like an eternity but was probably more along the line of minutes, light broke over Macy's face as the board was finally lifted away. Macy spotted Gabe first and while she was happy to see that the teenager was okay, she wanted to find Rhett's bright blues. She groaned, blinking hard, and took a shuddering breath.

Rhett was at her side in a heartbeat. "You have no idea. I thought—I feared—" He placed a hand on the small of her back as he assisted her with sitting up. "I've never been happier to see someone in my whole life."

Her lungs ached. Macy coughed a few times. "I heard you praying."

Rhett smiled gently. "I do that now."

Macy turned to say something more but Kodiak chose that moment to lurch toward Rhett so she could cover every inch of his face and neck with happy dog kisses. She whined and then licked, whined and then licked. Her whole body trembling.

Rhett's laugh was pure joy. A tear slipped down his cheek as he kissed the top of Kodiak's head. "Good girl. You are such a good girl, Kodiak. You heard my whistle, didn't you? You barked so well. That's how we found you."

Kodiak inched closer to Rhett and then let out one sharp yelp. Rhett's eyes went wide.

Macy sucked in another shuddering breath. "She's hurt. It's one of her back legs, I think."

Rhett's eyes found hers.

"Rubble fell on her. She was pinned."

Rhett's blue gaze raked over Macy's face, her body. "You're hurt too." He lightly touched her face. "You're covered in blood."

"I'm okay." Macy smiled despite the situation. "I love you, Rhett Jarrett. I don't want another second to go by without saying that. I've loved you—"

Rhett's mouth was on hers before she could finish. He kissed her lightly, tenderly, as if he was afraid anything more would break her. But Macy needed more. She fisted her hands into his shirt and yanked him closer. Rhett's hat slid off his head as they deepened their kiss. Macy had almost died today, but this kiss? This kiss was life and air and love and acceptance—everything she'd ever wanted. She was caked in mud, blood and sweat. She was soaked through but none of it mattered.

Macy let go of Rhett's shirt so she could wrap her arms around his neck. She loved this man. She wanted to stay in his arms forever.

The sound of someone *loudly* clearing their throat finally broke them apart.

Gabe smirked at them. "I'm sorry to interrupt y'all but..." He shrugged and held Rhett's hat out to them.

Rhett accepted his hat but kept his other arm firmly around Macy's back, supporting her. He shoved his hat onto his head and then slipped his hand under her knees. With Macy snug in his arms he got to his feet. He looked over at Gabe, who was still smiling wickedly at them. "Think you're strong enough to carry Kodiak back to the house?"

Gabe rolled his eyes. "Mr. Jarrett, I don't 'think'—I *know*."

Macy rested her hand on Rhett's chest to get his attention. "I can walk."

Rhett's arms tightened. "I'm not letting you go." He looked back at Gabe. "She tolerates a fireman's carry well. Do you know what that is? Over the shoulders?"

Gabe dropped to his knees and helped Kodiak get positioned around his neck.

"Lift with your knees," Rhett instructed.

Kodiak's brow wrinkled and she looked over at Rhett and Macy as if she wanted to ask them if they were really going to allow this kid to do this to her, but Gabe rose with minimal wobbling and headed up the hill in the direction of the house.

When they were alone Macy studied Rhett's face. She wanted to scrub away the worried crease in his brow. He noticed she was staring and cocked an eyebrow.

"You found me," she said. She wrapped an arm more securely around his neck.

"I was so scared," he confessed in a small voice.

"It was like our old hide-and-seek days."

His arms tightened. "I would have never stopped looking for you. I would have turned over every piece of rubble, searched in every place until I had you in my arms."

She tried to make light of it all, cheer him up. "Well, you won this round."

"Kodiak helped." Rhett took the hill slower. His gaze swept over Macy again. "I'm worried about this blood. Tell me what hurts."

"I'm alive, Rhett." Her laugh had a raw edge to it. Tiredness will do that. "What does it matter?"

Rhett stopped at the top of the hill and set her down on a wooden stool that must have been blown there from one of the barns.

He cupped her face in both his hands. "It matters because I love you. Everything about you matters to me. Every single thing." The muscle in his jaw popped. "When I thought… When I didn't know… When I couldn't find you…" He pressed his forehead to hers and took a long, slow breath. "I was such a fool not to say something sooner. Not to *do* something. I thought I had time. I thought we had time." He eased back again and brushed the hair out of her face that had fallen from her ponytail. "I love you so much, Macy. I'll spend the rest of my life trying to show you how much."

"Rhett." Her voice was barely a whisper. She was entirely overcome by the strength of his words.

"Now tell me what's hurt," he said.

He picked her back up and she told him about the projectile hitting her arm and the scratch on her face. "Other than that I think I'm just really sore."

Rhett had to step over wreckage all the way back to the house. Tears freely flowed down Macy's cheeks. Red Dog Ranch was completely destroyed. Finally unable emotionally to face the destruction any longer, Macy buried her face in Rhett's neck.

"It's all gone," she whispered. "Everything's gone."

She felt the muscles in his arms flex.

"Everything that matters made it," he murmured against her hair.

In the days after the tornado Rhett spent most of his time managing the cleanup effort. He kept a running list of things that needed to be replaced and repaired. The handwritten list currently covered ten pages, front and back. And it kept growing.

Jack Donnelley examined the two-story-tall,

boarded-up wall of the family room. "New windows coming this weekend?"

Rhett finished his tea and set the mug in the sink. "Yes, thankfully. It's a cave in here without them."

Jack crossed his arms. "Have you decided what to do about the rest of the property? All the cabins?"

Rhett pinched the bridge of his nose. "Honestly? I have no idea."

"Take it one day at a time," Jack said. "And no matter what you decide, my family and I will be here to support you."

"Even if I did away with Camp Firefly?" Rhett didn't know why he had tossed the question out there. Jack had come to know God because of Camp Firefly. The program meant the world to him. Of course he would want Rhett to reinstate it. But the cabins had been leveled and he'd been told it could take months for the insurance money to come through. So unless someone dropped a bundle of money and a crew of hundreds of workers on their doorstep, the ranch wouldn't be ready to host visitors for a long time.

Summer was only six weeks away.

"Like I said." Jack pulled on the gloves he wore to sift through rubble. The man had

been stopping by in his off-hours to volunteer. "Whatever you decide, we care about your family, Rhett. You Jarretts might as well be cousins as far as I'm concerned. I want whatever is best for you guys and only you can make that decision."

Rhett thanked Jack before he headed outside, and not for the first time Rhett regretted how he had treated the man in the past. Jack had proved to be an invaluable help and an even better friend. Because of the man's position with the Texas Department of Public Safety he was able to schedule relief workers, and since Red Dog Ranch had been the hardest hit out of anywhere, many of the volunteers were being diverted to them. Jack had been instrumental in coordinating transportation, food and lodging on the day of the tornado for all the remaining guests who had attended the fund-raising supper. He had also opened his house to Shannon and Rhett's mom for the time being. Rhett had chosen to stay in his family's house while the work was being done.

Lives had been lost in the tornado, but none of the casualties had occurred at Red Dog Ranch. It was something Rhett found himself thanking God for multiple times a day. The morning after the storm they had held an im-

promptu church service in the small chapel near the mess hall, which had made it through the tornado completely unscathed. Rhett and the staff had sung worship songs together and had prayed and thanked God for His protection.

Rhett's property was mostly totaled, seven of his horses were missing, and at least an eighth of his cattle had perished, but Macy's arm wound and a ranch hand with a broken leg had been the worst of their injuries. Much to Piper's dismay no one had been able to locate Sheep and Romeo, which Rhett knew Macy felt terrible about, but they hadn't found their bodies yet either so Rhett kept reminding both of them that there was hope.

When Rhett finally decided to go into the office and assess the damages there, Kodiak tried to limp beside him, but the full cast on her back leg slowed her down considerably. Rhett sighed. He felt sorry for her. She couldn't go in the water, couldn't play fetch, couldn't do any of the things that she loved.

"Ah, ah, you." Rhett picked his dog up and carried her back to the front porch of the family home. "I know it eats you up, but you have to stay off that leg. Don't look at me with those sad eyes. Doctor's orders." He set her gently on the large dog bed he had hauled out there for her minutes ago.

Kodiak harrumphed loudly but she laid her head down.

"Stay," Rhett commanded her. She had undergone surgery the night of the tornado and had had her back leg casted. Rhett had spent the night with her at the emergency vet clinic and hadn't slept a wink.

He still felt drained but he wasn't sure if it was from not enough sleep or all the stress. More than likely it was a hefty mix of the two.

Rhett had worked fourteen-to sixteen-hour days since the storm and during that time he had put off going to the office. He had told himself it was because there were plenty of other physical needs to attend to. Why should he spend time in the books when there were things to fix and repair? The office had been unreachable for the first forty-eight hours due to the fact that the tornado had seen fit to redecorate the building by dropping a bus on the front half of it. Rhett hadn't been allowed in there until someone from the city had approved the structure.

They had done so yesterday morning but Rhett had found other tasks to keep him busy.

In truth, he had avoided it because it had

been his father's domain and Rhett had faced so many losses and setbacks, he wasn't sure he could handle seeing the rest of his father's possessions destroyed.

But it was time.

The bus had smashed into Macy's section of the office so Rhett approached the back door, which led directly into his study. It was the door Macy had admonished him for sneaking out through that first night. Rhett sucked in a deep breath and then eased the door open. He was instantly hit with a strong musty scent. His dad's books were scattered all over the room. The large desk was still in its place and for some reason that was enough to coax Rhett the rest of the way into the space. There was plenty of water damage from a large gap in the wall near the roof. Most of his dad's papers were shot.

Rhett's throat burned as he assessed the area.

Each smashed book, every scattered page and broken picture frame felt like another piece of his dad being taken away. He hadn't mourned his father properly when he passed, but Rhett let the full impact of his death rest on him now as he stood in his father's demolished office.

His dad was gone. The thought hollowed him out just as much as the first time he had thought those words. Brock had been gone for more than a month, but knowing and accepting were two very different processes. Rhett would rebuild, but he would make it his own. The traces that had made it feel as if Brock was simply gone on an errand and would return later—all of that was gone.

On the other side of the room the painting his mom had created of a herd of longhorns hung half off the wall, and there was another gaping hole in the wood paneling behind it. His mom had given the painting to his father as a Valentine's day gift and Brock had cherished the thing. When Rhett still called Red Dog Ranch home not a week had elapsed without Brock gesturing at the painting and saying something like, "Look at that picture, my boy. That right there, it holds the secret to the most important thing in my life." Rhett had always assumed his dad meant his wife. Marriage.

Rhett made his way across the room to adjust the painting but the hook was gone. In fact… He lifted the painting away and balanced it on a chair to keep it away from the water. There was something behind the painting. What looked like a small fireproof chamber was built into the wall, perfectly concealed behind the painting. He pulled on the small handle and the door swung open to reveal a shoebox tucked inside. Rhett drew the box out.

Heart pounding, he carried it to the desk and sat down. He opened the lid and the contents made his fingers shake as he tried to make sense of what was inside. A little stuffed red dog that was somehow familiar even though Rhett couldn't remember ever seeing it before. And paperwork. An adoption certificate with his name and the names Brock and Leah Jarrett. His parents.

But it didn't make sense.

Rhett dug into the box again and found pictures. A baby in a blue onesie sleeping next to the red stuffed dog. A baby laughing while he clutched the little red stuffed animal. He carefully flipped each one over and, sure enough, someone had written the dates on the backs. The pictures were of him. There were more papers in the box but Rhett didn't know if he could handle what he might find. He braced an elbow on either side of the box, pressed a hand to each of his temples and stared at the contents. Spots flashed in his vision. He felt like a fish that had just been torn from the water and was left gasping for air.

Brock and Leah weren't his biological parents. Rhett's head pounded.

The back door to his office creaked on its hinges.

"Rhett!" Macy burst in. "We found them! Sheep and Romeo. They were at the old Tennison Pond."

Rhett never took his eyes off the certificate of adoption. "That's great. Real great." He spoke with no voice inflection.

"Are you all right?" She stopped a few feet away.

Rhett ran trembling fingers over his jaw. "I'm not sure."

Macy stepped closer. She scanned the desk and breathed, "Brock wanted to tell you. He loved you, Rhett."

Rhett's head snapped up. "Did you know?"

Macy held up her hands. "Let me explain."

"For how long?" He ground out the words.

Her gaze darted away from his. She licked her lips. "It's been less than two years."

"*Two years?*" Rhett shot to his feet. He jabbed at the adoption certificate. *His* adoption certificate. "You've known for two years that I was adopted and you kept it from me? How could you do that to me?"

She flinched and took a step back. "I had to, Rhett. Please."

Rhett fought the rash urge to hurtle the shoebox across the room. Did everyone know? Was it some joke, some great prank they thought they could play with his life? He was thirty years old and just finding out the truth.

They had lied to him. His whole life. It had all been a lie.

He wasn't a Jarrett.

Macy's shoe crunched on some of the wreckage in the office and the sound brought Rhett swiftly back into his surroundings.

Rhett released a rattling breath. "I'd like you to leave."

"Hear me out."

"Right now." He worked his jaw back and forth. "Please, just leave me alone."

"Rhett."

"I don't want to talk to you about this. Not now."

He needed some time. Needed to process. Needed to be alone.

He braced his hands on the desk and sank back into his chair. He suddenly felt very tired and very drained and Rhett didn't think he could have kept standing if he had wanted to.

He focused on the chamber in the wall that had hidden Brock's secret.

Rhett heard the door open again. Heard slow footsteps. Then nothing.

She was gone and he told himself it was for the best.

Chapter Twelve

"All right." Sophie Donnelley dried off the last cup, set it in a cupboard then pivoted to face Macy. She leaned against the counter. "We've left you to your own devices long enough. It's time to spill."

Macy hugged her middle as she considered how best to dodge the conversation Sophie clearly wanted to have. "I don't know what you're talking about."

Not true.

I'd like you to leave.

I don't want to talk to you about this.

Rhett's words flew through her mind like they had a hundred times since she left Red Dog Ranch. Guilt had draped itself around Macy, weighing her down. She had held a piece of truth about Rhett's life and had kept it from him.

In thirty-six hours Rhett hadn't called her. Hadn't texted.

She wouldn't blame him if he never forgave her.

That day she had sat in her bungalow for an hour before deciding the only way to give Rhett the space he needed would be to actually leave the property. Red Dog Ranch had been her home for the last ten years and before that it had been her second home. All her friends were tied to the ranch in some way. Most of them lived on the property.

After packing a bag, initially she hadn't known where to go. She could have rented a hotel room in town, but she'd ended up absently driving around for a while. Intermittently switching between praying, turning up her music, pulling over to cry, praying some more. Without really meaning to she had finally ended up pulling into the Donnelleys' driveway.

Macy had almost left but Jack had happened to arrive home at the same time, and he had let her know that Shannon and Mrs. Jarrett had moved back to their property a few hours earlier because the windows had been installed and the power was back on. Then he'd told Macy he and Sophie wouldn't hear of her going anywhere else as he'd ushered her inside.

"Nice try." Sophie draped the dish towel over her shoulder. She eyed Macy the same way Macy had seen her stare down her children when they needed a talking to. "Spill whatever it was that brought you to our door in tears yesterday with your belongings. Let's start there."

She couldn't evade the Donnelleys' questions forever. Talking was inevitable. Besides, Macy had never been one to hold in her words.

Except about Rhett's origins.

Except for the *one time* she most definitely should have talked.

Macy gestured toward the table. "We should sit first."

"Jack and the kids are zonked out already so we can talk all night if you need to." Sophie joined her there a few minutes later with two cups of sweet tea in hand. Macy told Sophie about when Rhett left the ranch and their first kiss. Then she shared about how she and Rhett had been treating each other like boyfriend and girlfriend ever since the storm.

"I've loved him for so long and we've been through so much but…but I kept something really important from Rhett. Something he deserved to know." Macy decided that Sophie didn't need to hear every detail of the secret she'd kept from Rhett for her to understand and give advice. Besides, Rhett had only just learned he was adopted and now it was his right to tell or not tell people as he chose.

There had been a time when Macy had almost asked Uncle Travis if he knew the truth, but she hadn't been able to think of a way to broach the subject without revealing what she knew. If Travis did know, he had never said anything.

When Macy finished telling her story, her chest felt empty, completely hollowed out. It had taken more than an hour and two refills of sweet tea to explain everything.

Sophie tapped a finger on the table. "When he asked you to leave—"

"*Told* me to leave."

Sophie arched an eyebrow. "He told you, like a command?"

"I'm not sure, actually." Macy shoved a hand through her hair. Her eyes hurt. She hadn't slept much last night. "It happened so fast."

And her guilt might have been adding to the story.

Sophie's head tilted in thought. She pursed

her lips then asked, "Did he say he wanted you gone forever?"

Rhett hadn't needed to say forever because Macy had seen it in the way he wouldn't make eye contact, in his broken posture. Trust was hard fought and easily broken in Rhett Jarrett's world.

"He won't want to see me again. Not after this," Macy said. "Last time it took three years before we spoke. With what I kept from him this time around?" Macy hugged her middle again. Maybe she could keep her heart from feeling as if it was slinking away to some cave to hide. Probably not. "This is far worse. This could be forever."

"You only feel like that in the moment. But it sounds like last time around you two didn't talk for three years for no other reason than you were both too stubborn and scared to return each other's calls. How about try being vulnerable this time around and reaching out—with the understanding, of course, that he may need some time to process and that's okay? Rhett taking time is not a rejection. You understand that, right?"

But Sophie didn't know what Macy had kept from Rhett. Macy had stumbled upon Rhett's adoption paperwork when Brock was having the fireproof chamber installed. She had begged Brock to tell Rhett, but Brock had insisted she promise not to tell him. Supposedly he had made a promise to Rhett's birth mother that Rhett would never know he was adopted.

Later Macy had wondered more about the circumstances of Rhett's birth. Why would a mother not want her child to know about his origins? She had approached Brock about it twice more within the first month of finding out, asking him to tell Rhett, but Brock had said he could never tell. He convinced Macy that Rhett would feel betrayed and could leave the family for good if he discovered the truth. With as divided as Rhett and Brock had been after Wade's death, Macy had hardly wanted a hand in driving them even further apart so against her better judgment she had agreed.

Sophie's voice broke through her thoughts. "Did Rhett actually say 'I don't want to see you again'?"

"He didn't have to." Macy's eyes burned. She needed to go to sleep. Needed to stop talking. "I really messed everything up, didn't I?"

"I wouldn't be so sure. Honestly, I feel like you're making some leaps based on assumptions." Sophie's lips tipped up encouragingly. "I know we haven't spoken much about it specifically, but you're a woman of faith, right?"

"I believe in God, yes." Macy uncurled her arms so she could trace a notch in the table. Her other hand moved to cup the cool glass of tea. "Actually, when I was stuck in the tornado I had this moment of revelation. You see, my entire life I've felt like I didn't measure up—not to my family, my friends or to God—but during that storm I realized that God's always loved me and I didn't have to do anything to earn His love."

"That's a wonderful knowledge to have, isn't it? There's a Bible verse we've been going over in the women's study group I'm a part of." Sophie thumbed through a stack of papers on the table that was full of kids' artwork. "I thought I had my notes here somewhere." She pushed the papers away. "I can't find the study sheet but the gist of it was that God never forsakes those who trust Him. The Bible mentions that truth many times. It's almost as if God knew we would need to hear it over and over before we believed it." Sophie smiled across the table. "God has not left you, He has not forsaken you and He will see you through this. Hang on to that."

Macy sighed. "God might be willing to ride this bumpy train with me, but what if Rhett's not?"

"I wouldn't lose faith in Rhett if I were you," Sophie said. "Give him time to absorb whatever it is he just learned about. Right now, be there for him in ways you can."

Macy's sharp laugh held no humor. "I don't think he wants me to be there for him at all."

"Nothing is stopping you from praying for him." Sophie winked. "And you're resourceful so I'm sure you'll think of other ways too." They cleared the table and both headed for bed but Sophie caught Macy's arm before she could turn toward the guest room. "Can I pray for you?"

"Of course." Macy took the other woman's hand. They bowed their heads and both ended up praying for Rhett and the ranch and each other.

"And thank You for never forsaking us. Never leaving. Thank You for loving us just as we are." Sophie squeezed Macy's hands. "Amen."

However, even after Macy was tucked away in the guest room for the night she was restless. It wasn't even late yet but the kids had an early bedtime and Jack had stumbled to his bedroom after tucking the kids in, saying he was running on empty. Macy put on her pajamas and got into bed but turned the light back on a few minutes later. What if Rhett or Shannon had sent an email? She dug through her things for her phone and her laptop.

She had a missed call but it was from Gabe the intern, not one of the Jarretts. "So, I know things aren't great right now," Gabe said in the message. "But I have an idea to help the ranch get back on its feet. Do you still have Clint Oakfield's number? Call me, okay?"

It wasn't late yet, but her throat was sore from talking with Sophie so she decided to call Gabe back in the morning. Gabe's call and her talk with Sophie worked together to shove Macy's brain into hyperdrive. Sophie was right; she didn't have to be at the ranch to help and support them. And she didn't need Rhett's approval to help. God had placed Red Dog Ranch in her life and she would fight to rebuild it however she could.

Macy opened her laptop and did a quick internet search for crowdfunding sites. She let her cursor hover over the top site for only a heartbeat before she clicked it. *Do it. Do it before you can think better of it.* It took her fifteen minutes to set up a page asking for donations; most of that time was spent typing out a passionate and heartfelt plea in which she detailed the storm's destruction, as well as all the amazing programs the ranch offered free of charge to foster families. She mentioned Rhett's desire to train therapy dogs, as well. She prayed her love for her favorite place shined through. When it was done she pressed for the page to go live before she could convince herself not to. With two clicks she linked the donation page to two of her social media accounts and then slammed her laptop closed.

Macy flipped off the lights and curled back into bed.

Had she just made another colossal mistake? Would her actions serve to drive Rhett further away? No, she'd done what she knew was right, what God would want her to do, and she could live with that.

Macy loved Rhett. No matter what happened, she always would.

But if the past few weeks had taught Macy anything, it was that she couldn't build her life on one person or one place or even one mission. She could only build her life on God and what God would have her do.

And that would be enough.

* * *

Rhett—

I'm writing this because Macy keeps insisting you deserve to know and you deserve answers. I suppose if this is in your hands then you moved your mom's painting and I'm sure you have a heap of questions. Why would your mom and I keep something like this from you? Why did we work so hard to ensure you wouldn't discover the truth? You have every right to be upset and angry. I don't blame you for either. I do hope you can find it within you to forgive an old fool.

You and me have been at odds ever since we lost Wade, and I don't know how to put that to right. I think if I would have told you the truth about your adoption I might have lost you too, and I couldn't have borne that.

Years ago your mother and I were volunteering at a youth group when we met your birth mom. She was scared and alone and she knew she couldn't keep you, but she loved you with such a protective love. I want you to know that, Rhett—you have never lived a day when you weren't fiercely loved by your birth mother, by me and your mom and by God. She had grown up in the system and it had failed her. A family had adopted her, but they'd always made her feel secondhand and more as live-in help than a branch in their tree.

She dreamed bigger for you. You've always reminded me of her in that way. When we told her we wanted to adopt you, that you were an answer to our prayers, she made us promise to treat you as our flesh and blood. We would have anyway, but the promise was important to her, and your mom and I are people of our word.

Perhaps I should own up to a more selfish reason too. From the first day you were in my arms you were my child, Rhett. I never saw you as anything but a Jarrett. I was a sentimental fool who wanted it to always stay that way. When you chose to leave us I told myself that you would have left sooner had you known, so then I guarded the secret even more doggedly.

For that I'm sorry.

Now you know our secret, but I can't go any further. We promised your biological mother if you ever did discover you were adopted, we would still protect her identity. She gave you the red stuffed dog you loved so well. You carried that thing everywhere your first few years.

If you haven't figured it out by now, your mom and I walked away from the life we had once we adopted you. We used Grandpa Jarrett's oil money to purchase this ranch. I didn't know a thing about cattle! But I did know I wanted to help kids. You opened my heart up to this life— to all of life. Every choice after that was made because of our great love for you. You filled our hearts and our lives with so much joy it overflowed. We wanted to give that joy to others, so we created a safe place for foster children to enjoy—a place that could feel like a second home.

Red Dog Ranch has been and always will be a symbol of our love for you. You made us parents. You made us a family. We are forever grateful for the gift of you. I'm so proud of you and the man you have become, son.

With all the love in my heart,
Dad

Each time Rhett reread the letter he felt something different. At first it was anger and betrayal but that faded into shades of acceptance tipped with disappointment.

Was it possible to track down his birth mother?

Did he want to?

Rhett hardly knew.

Folding the paper back up, Rhett tucked it into the pocket on his shirt where it would be close to his heart. He rested his hands on the edge of his belt as he looked out the newly installed floor-to-ceiling windows of the family room. Moonlight rippled over the large lake that sprawled behind the Jarrett family home. They had dredged the last of the debris from the lake yesterday morning and Rhett found he was glad he had moved that task up the prioritized list. The lake was a special place for him.

Red Dog Ranch has been and always will be a symbol of our love for you.

A lump formed in the back of Rhett's throat. He rubbed a fist over his collarbone to try to dispel the feeling, but it lingered. Maybe it always would.

He had been so bitter over this place, so wrong.

His phone vibrated in his back pocket and as he fished it out he wildly hoped it was Macy. Rhett owed her an apology. He was still upset about her keeping such a huge secret from him, but he shouldn't have pushed her away.

When he asked her to go, he had meant he needed a few hours to himself. When Shannon told him Macy had left the ranch, Rhett had figured she had wanted some space too and he had respected that by not bothering her with calls. But when her car hadn't appeared today, Rhett had started to worry. Had his words driven her away?

Rhett didn't know where she was staying. The few times he had worked up the nerve to call her today, her phone had been off and her voice mail was oddly full.

He would find her at some point and he would ask her to come home. He couldn't run the place without her. He wanted her around, near him.

He glanced at his phone screen: Boone.

Boone blinked at him over the face-to-face connection program on their phones. Rhett had talked with most of his family about being adopted, but he hadn't been able to catch his brother yet.

"How's the ranch doing?"

"It's a mess." If only he was exaggerating.

"The pictures you sent of the damage turned my stomach. We wish we were there to help,"

Boone said. "Oh, and before I forget, I'm supposed to tell you June and Hailey say hi."

Rhett's brother Boone had met his wife, June, in high school. They had always joked about their names rhyming and had teased that they would pick their kids' names to rhyme, as well. When Hailey was born there was speculation about what her name would be… Thankfully they went against the rhyming scheme.

Rhett's watch showed that it was after eleven in Maine where Boone and his family lived. He chuckled softly. "I'm sure they're both long asleep by now so tell them hi in the morning for me."

"We keep late hours in seminary." Boone's yawn followed quickly.

Rhett glanced over at his mom asleep in her recliner and Kodiak snoozing near his mom's feet. "There's something I need to tell you." Rhett plunged right in and told Boone about discovering the shoebox in their dad's office and explained what he had found inside.

Boone was quiet when Rhett paused, but finally he let out a low whistle. "Wow. That's a lot to deal with all at once. How are you holding up?"

"Boone." Something had been bothering Rhett since he had learned about being adopted and he had to get it off his chest. "You're technically the oldest Jarrett. Dad's will names you as the heir in the event that something happens to me or if I'm unable to serve as director." Rhett heard Boone make a disgruntled noise on the other end of the line so he rushed on. "This inheritance… I know you said you don't want to run the ranch, but if that ever changes, if you ever want to take this from me—"

But it wasn't Boone who answered Rhett first. It was their mom.

"Why, that's the daftest thing I've ever heard you say." His mom pounded her hand on her armrest. Evidently she hadn't been sleeping all that deeply after all. Kodiak's head swung up. She sleepily blinked in Rhett's general direction.

Rhett turned up the volume on his phone. "Mom's on with us."

Their mom curled her finger, a silent command for Rhett to draw closer. He obeyed. He crossed over to her and knelt at her feet.

She cupped his cheek in her weatherworn hand. "You are my firstborn son. It doesn't matter that someone else bore you—you were my first child, my first little love." She ran her thumb in a light caress over his skin. "God knew you were the brother Boone, Wade and

Shannon needed. And He knew you were the son who would first make me a mother. No secret, no hurt can make any of those things untrue."

Rhett swallowed hard.

"This family has loved you and prayed for you and cheered for you since before you were even born. You are ours, child. Ours," his mom continued more firmly. "And you always will be."

Boone's face lighted up Rhett's phone screen. "I'm one hundred percent going with Mom on this one."

"Smart boy." Their mom beamed at both of them.

The front door opened and Shannon tiptoed in. She started when she spotted them in the family room. "Way to scare a girl silly! You guys are still awake?"

"Join us." Rhett motioned for her to come over. "We're on with Boone."

"Aww, Boone! My favorite middle brother." Shannon shrugged off her purse and skidded across the wood floor to sit beside Rhett. She tossed an arm over his shoulder and reached to hold her mom's hand in her other. Rhett eased back so he was sitting on his ankles. He kept the phone so Boone could see all three of them.

Rhett took a deep breath. "Since I have most of the family here I'd like to ask for some advice." They were missing Cassidy, but she and Piper had their own house on the property and they would be asleep by now.

Mom's brow bunched together. Her gaze darted around the room as if she was searching for a lost item. "Where are Brock and Wade? Do we need to wake them?"

Boone's focus went to Rhett and Shannon. "I, ah, I think this is plenty of us for an opinion."

Rhett had worried that the family gathering might confuse his mother. He needed to be more careful with how he phrased things.

"As everyone here knows, the ranch suffered heavy damages. Besides our barns, Camp Firefly—mainly the cabins—was the hardest hit part of our land." Although that didn't mean a whole lot. The tornado had carved a path from one end of his property line to the other. As if the storm had wanted to wage a war on Rhett specifically. Much of the ranch looked like it had been walloped with a meat tenderizer. "Now we need to decide what we're going to do."

Shannon's fingers tightened on his shoulder. "Wait. You're not planning to rebuild?"

Rhett looked away from them and worked his jaw a few times. "We don't have enough money. Insurance only helps to a point and even if they end up helping more, it won't be quickly enough to host camp." He spoke slowly, evenly delivering the information so everyone understood what they were facing. "At the least, I think we need to consider cancelling this summer."

"We can't." Shannon sat up a little more, letting go of their mom's hand in the process.

"If God wants our mission to continue, He will find a way." Their mom rested her hands in her lap. "You'll see."

Rhett rubbed his jaw. "Everyone made it through the storm safe. I think we should be grateful with that huge blessing from God and not expect a bunch more."

"Do you think there's a cap to how much love God can shower on us?" Their mom laughed gently. "Do you think He ever says, 'Oh, that's enough, I'll stop showing them my love'?" Mom leaned forward and whispered, "God delights in loving us. Don't forget that."

Shannon bit her lip and sought Rhett's eyes. "What about the family holdings?"

"That money is for the family to live off of." Rhett sliced his hand through the air. His heart had changed toward the foster programs, but he was still firm in his belief that the business account shouldn't mix with the family's personal money. "That's the legacy I want to leave to my nieces."

Boone spoke up first. "Legacy isn't money—you know that, right?"

"Boone's right." Shannon's fingers drew across his back as she leaned away from him. "The Jarrett family legacy is this ranch and what this ranch stands for."

Rhett knew that. He did. But he also knew that he had some tough business decisions ahead of him.

"Your nieces don't need you to worry about leaving them with a nest egg." Boone straightened in his chair. Rhett had to bite back a smile because he could tell Boone was about to launch into what they called his pastor mode. Boone had always been the bookish one in the family.

"The Bible talks a lot about treasures in heaven," Boone said. "Meaning we should be doing things that please God instead of amassing things here on earth." His hand came into view. "Now, I don't think that means that we don't take care of our family or make sound business choices. But I do think when we use the word *legacy*, as Christians it should only ever be in the realm of a legacy for the Kingdom. What are we devoting our time and energy and resources on earth to? Things that matter in eternity or not?"

"You do know you're not a minister yet, right?" Shannon teased.

They laughed and the conversation turned to catching up, but Rhett was unable to keep his mind from wandering. It wasn't the first time he had considered how people would remember him after he was gone someday. As morbid as it sounded, it was something that had crossed his mind often since his father had passed away.

How did Rhett want to be remembered?

As a man who took care of his family or someone who ran a successful business? Why couldn't he be both? But as the voices of his family—the family God had chosen for him— drifted over him, Rhett knew his answer was neither of those things. It didn't have to be one or the other.

Rhett would choose God.

He would trust God with the ranch and with his family.

He would hand it over. All of it.

Chapter Thirteen

"Rhett!" Shannon pounded on his bedroom door. "Rhett Jarrett, you need to get out of bed this instant and come downstairs."

Rhett groaned and sat up slowly. After they had hung up with Boone last night Rhett had headed outside to pray and clear his head. He had ended up staying up until past two in the morning and was not yet ready to handle any amount of his sister's exuberance.

Although it was nice to catch a glimpse of the old Shannon again. She was still dating Cord, and Rhett was praying about how he should deal with their relationship. Rhett knew for sure that Cord was no good for his sister, but his sister was an adult and he couldn't force her to break up with someone either.

He glanced at his clock and discovered to

his embarrassment that his family had let him sleep until noon.

"Open up now, Rhett. I mean it." She kept knocking. "Or I'll barge in and pour water over your head like when we were kids."

"I'm up," he muttered. He raked his hand down his face then rose. "And if I remember correctly, you got in trouble for that."

"Worth it," she called through the door.

Rhett grinned and crossed the room. Good thing it was only his sister because he usually wouldn't wander out of his room in his old sweatpants and undershirt. He pulled open the door and had to shield his eyes against the sunlight streaming into the hallway through the wide glass panels in the window seat. "So where's the fire?"

Shannon latched onto his wrist and tugged him over the threshold. "The place is swimming with reporters. They're all asking for you. I tried to hold them off but they keep showing up."

Reporters?

That didn't make any sense.

Rhett caught the ridge of trim around his door so she couldn't tug him forward anymore. "Slow down. What are you talking about?"

"Downstairs." She trained both of her

pointer fingers downward. "Some from the papers and a couple from the internet. There are even ones out there with camera crews and they all want to see your pretty mug." She let go of him and pursed her lips. "Oh, you need to change. Maybe shower too?" She pulled a face. "No, that will take too long." She put her fingertips on his chest and gave him a push back toward his room. "Go make yourself presentable."

"Call me slow, but I'm not following any of this." Rhett crossed his arms. "Why would reporters have any interest in talking to me?"

Shannon gave a long suffering huff and tapped on her phone. She pulled open a webpage and shoved the phone in his face. "This is why."

Rhett jerked his head back and snatched the phone from her so he could hold it at an angle where he could see the screen. A picture of Sheep and Romeo was splashed across the top of the page.

Fund-raiser by Macy Howell: Red Dog Ranch

The bar showing donations was already past its goal and a small flag in the corner announced that it was a trending fund-raiser.

The page went on to talk about all the lives the ranch had touched and changed, Macy's included.

This place is home not just to the generous family that runs it free of charge to participants, but it becomes home to every foster child who steps onto the ranch. It's the only taste of home some kids ever know. When I was a lost child it became my home too.

She went on to explain all the free programs offered at Red Dog Ranch, followed that with detailing the destruction wrought by the tornado and ended with a call to action.

I've known the ranch's amazing owner, Rhett Jarrett, all my life and he's the one who taught me long ago to dream big, impossible dreams, so I've placed the amount we need to raise high. There are only weeks left until camp starts. Will you dream big with us?

Rhett's throat burned with emotion. "I need to find her."

"What you need to do—" Shannon grabbed his shoulders, turned him slightly and guided him all the way into his room "—is change and deal with all these people waiting in our dining room."

"You're right." Rhett crossed to his closet and pulled a fresh shirt off a hanger. "But when I'm done with them, I'm going to figure out where she went."

"Macy?" Shannon cocked her head. "Oh, she's over at the Donnelleys'."

Rhett's mouth was probably wide open. "Jack told you but not me?"

"No." She batted the suggestion away. "It took me all of ten seconds of thought to realize that Macy literally had nowhere to go but the Donnelleys' unless she went to one of the hotels. I guessed." Shannon shrugged. "I went there a few hours after she left and sure enough, there she was."

Jack hadn't said a word. Not that Rhett had told his new friend that he was trying to find Macy, but it was curious that her staying at their house hadn't come up. Then again, Rhett hadn't confided in Jack about what had happened between the two of them. Additionally, Macy very well may have asked the Donnelleys not to tell anyone she was staying there and the Donnelleys would have honored her request.

Just like his parents had honored his birth mom's request.

Still, Shannon had figured out Macy's whereabouts when he hadn't put two and two together. "I can't believe I didn't figure that out."

Shannon didn't even attempt to hide her eye roll. "Seriously, Rhett, where else would she have gone?"

Nowhere.

The thought gutted him.

Red Dog Ranch was her home—her world. And he had unintentionally shoved her out in the cold.

"I need to apologize to her."

Shannon's answering laugh was quick and sharp. "Oh, you need to do a lot more than that."

He scrubbed his hand down his face. "I never told her to leave the ranch. It was a miscommunication."

"And then some," Shannon said.

"Point made." He held his hands out.

"My advice?" She sauntered into the hallway. "A lot of groveling, some pleading and definitely kneeling down when you beg that woman to marry you, okay?"

Rhett swallowed a few times and then nodded. "I will."

"Get her back, Rhett. She's family."

He smiled at his sister and then he shut the door so he could get ready.

The afternoon flew by in a blur of interviews and phone calls. Not only had Macy's online fund-raiser gone viral, but Clint Oakfield had penned a blog entry about his experience at the ranch when the tornado hit and he had shared it everywhere he had an online presence. He expressed how he cared about the vision of Red Dog Ranch and he implored his fans to stand behind the rebuilding efforts. People in the comment section were offering to donate supplies or put together teams of free labor. Clint ended his post with a promise to host a benefit concert with all proceeds going to support the ranch's foster programs. He pledged to partner with Rhett and the ranch for as long as they would let him.

Once the first interview aired they had to forward the office line to the house phone and Shannon was flooded with incoming calls.

"How does Macy handle this all day? I can't answer these fast enough." Shannon set the phone down to refill her water. "Everyone wants our address so they can send checks. People are planning workdays and wanting to coordinate the best way to help. Our voice-mail box has already reached capacity!"

Cars started showing up in the driveway full of people who wanted to hand Rhett a check or drop off construction materials. There were crews lined up to begin rebuilding the cabins starting next week.

Rhett had never said thank-you so many times in his life. It was overwhelming.

God delights in loving us. Don't forget that.

He should have known better than to doubt his mom's wisdom. God's love had no cap, no end. Rhett felt like he was flooded in blessings, but instead of wondering like usual when it all would end or if there would be a trade-off, he was simply thankful.

Uncle Travis had reminded Rhett about the Bible verse that said to whom much is given, much is required. At the time Travis had been talking about Brock's will. But Rhett had been given an inheritance far greater than three thousand acres of gorgeous Texas Hill Country. God had given Rhett an inheritance of love—the deep and abiding, never-giving-up type of love that no man could ever hope to deserve. He had been given much and he would spend the rest of his life making sure every person who stepped onto his property got to experience the same love too.

And he needed to start with Macy.

Macy had spent most of the day staring at her computer screen in shocked awe as she witnessed the donation amount grow. She hadn't expected it to catch fire overnight quite like it had. Of course it was a good thing—Red Dog Ranch would have an opportunity to rebuild faster and return more quickly to being a safe haven for hurting kids.

Macy slammed her laptop closed and slung her purse over her shoulder. It was time to go to the ranch. She wasn't going to sit around waiting for three years like last time.

Macy burst out the Donnelleys' front door and charged directly into a solid chest. Hands took hold of her arms, steadying her. Rhett's handsome face—his strong jaw and shocking blue eyes—came into view and her heart squeezed. She loved this man.

She needed a little space so she would be able to say the things she had planned to.

Macy shrugged out of his hold. "Jack's not home."

Rhett eyed her. "I'm here for you."

Trying not to let his words derail her, Macy

gripped on to her purse strap as if it was a life-line. "I'm going to take an educated guess and assume you know what I've done?"

Rhett took off his hat and worked it around in his hands. His hair stuck up in the odd, adorable way it always did. "If you mean I need to thank you for single-handedly saving the ranch, then yes, I know about that. And I'm forever indebted to you for doing so." He looked down at his hat. "I wouldn't have acted that swiftly or even thought to take that measure." He peeked at her with a tentative smile on his face. "You sure know how to take on the world and win. I'm glad I have you in my corner…that is, if you still want to be."

It took every ounce of her restraint not to close the gap between them. "I should have told you about being adopted. I should have told you when I first found the paperwork. I'm so sorry, Rhett. You have no idea how sorry I am."

"Why didn't you tell me?"

She wove her fingers together. "I looked up to Brock so much. I think I had him on a bit of a pedestal. He was there for me when I had no parents." She shrugged. "A part of me felt like I owed him for letting me live here and giving me a job and basically giving me a family

too. Selfishly I didn't want to jeopardize that."
She rushed on, "And you and I weren't speaking, and when you came here we avoided each other so I convinced myself it wasn't my secret to tell—that you wouldn't have wanted to hear it from me anyway."

He nodded his understanding.

Macy sucked in a breath. "And I didn't want to drive you further away from your family either. Brock was really afraid of that happening." She took a half step closer. "I should have said something when you got back to the ranch."

His eyes searched hers.

"But I held on to this idea that I had to honor Brock by keeping the secret. As if it was even more important since he was gone. That probably sounds stupid, but I feel so much loyalty to him and I'm sorry. I'm so sorry and I don't know how I can even ask you to forgive me for keeping something so huge from you, but I am. Is this something we can get through?"

He reached toward her, slipped a piece of hair behind her ear. He left his hand there to cup her face as he said, "I'm pretty sure we can get through anything as long as we're together."

Macy pressed her cheek into his hand. "I

thought about telling you so many times and I came close but—"

"But you're a woman of your word—one of the many things I love about you—so you kept a promise to a man who was like a father to you." Rhett's voice was full of tenderness. "I see only someone doing something admirable. You have nothing to apologize for." He splayed his other hand over his heart. "I'm sorry I told you to leave."

"You had every right."

The muscles along his jaw stretched taut. "I only wanted an hour to collect my thoughts. I never thought you would take it as me asking you to leave the ranch. Please." He rested his forehead against hers. "Don't ever leave again."

"Never," she whispered.

He stepped back, set his hat on and thumbed toward his truck. "I brought someone else who wanted to see you." He whistled and Kodiak's head popped through the window. Her tail wagging was evident from where Macy stood.

Macy couldn't help but smile at seeing Kodiak. "How's she doing?"

"Good, but she misses you." Rhett stepped into her line of vision again.

"Wait. Rhett." Macy grabbed his arm. "I

forgot to tell you. There's this organization in California that specializes in training therapy dogs and they caught wind of our fund-raiser. They reached out to me with an offer for you. They want to fly you out there for a week or two this fall so you can learn their methods and connect with their trainers. I think it would be amazing."

Rhett's mouth opened, closed, opened again. "I feel like this is the right moment to say I finally understand the phrase 'my cup runneth over.'"

Macy held out her hand. "Should we head home?"

"Well, we actually need to talk about that." Rhett took her hand. "See, I don't want you back as the assistant."

Macy's heart plummeted. Had she heard him wrong? "But, Rhett, I—"

"I want to hire you as my codirector," Rhett said. "Equal decision-making power."

"Codirector of the ranch," said Macy, trying out the title. "Are you kidding?"

"I've never been more sure of anything in my life. I can't run the ranch without you. But more than that." He took a step forward and held out his other hand so they were facing one another again. "I need you in my life. I want you beside me in all things."

She slipped her hand into his. "Rhett."

He glanced at her lips and then met her eyes. "I can't promise a perfect life or even an easy one, but I can promise to love you every day for the rest of my life."

"I never wanted perfect." She brought their joined hands up between them. Macy looked into his eyes and knew she wanted to wake up to the sight of him every morning. "I only ever wanted you."

He let go of her hands only to slip his fingers into her hair. "I love you, Macy."

Macy tipped her face up. "I love you too."

Last time his kiss had been slow and gentle, but this kiss was sure and full of tomorrows. This kiss proclaimed love and promises. He angled his head to deepen their kiss at the same time she tiptoed her fingers to the hair at the nape of his neck. When they finally came up for air they both just grinned at each other.

His expression instantly sobered. "Macy, I don't have a ring. I thought of a speech on the way over but I'm so nervous it's fled. Will you—"

"Of course I'll marry you." Heart full, Macy laughed and tugged him close for another kiss. It was a quick peck that left her wanting ten more. She moved in for another but then stopped. "I interrupted you again, didn't I? And in the middle of... I'm sorry, Rhett, I couldn't help it. I've been waiting to be able to give you my answer for years."

"A few more kisses and we'll call it even." He winked.

"I like your terms." She playfully jabbed him in the ribs.

They climbed into his truck but Macy only scooted so far as the middle seat of the bench so Kodiak could stay sprawled with her cast in the passenger seat. Kodiak laid her head on Macy's thigh and let out a long, contented sigh. When Rhett got in, Macy looped her arm through his. He pressed another kiss to her temple and pointed the truck in the direction of Red Dog Ranch.

Toward home.

* * * * *

*Don't miss upcoming books in
Jessica Keller's Red Dog Ranch miniseries
from Love Inspired!*

*And enjoy these other Western stories
by Jessica Keller:*

Home for Good
The Ranger's Texas Proposal

Dear Reader,

Have you ever been faced with a situation you weren't sure you could handle?

Rhett didn't feel equipped to lead Red Dog Ranch and definitely didn't want to be compared to his father. At first he only saw his inheritance as a burden to escape from, but later on he was able to see it for the blessing it was in his life. I'm so glad he found a way to share his load so he could honor his father's wishes while still pursuing his dream of training dogs.

I think my favorite conversation in the book is when Mrs. Jarrett asks Rhett if he believes there's a cap on how much love God can shower on us. I really identified with Rhett in that moment. It's so difficult not to question and wonder and feel inadequate.

But God delights in loving us. Don't forget that.

Thank you for spending time with Rhett and Macy. I hope you enjoyed their story as much as I enjoyed writing it. Make sure to look up the rest of the Red Dog Ranch series—each one follows one of the Jarrett siblings.

Dream big,
Jess